SUPER DOLL

ERIN SCHULZ

WS BEETLE
& COMPANY

Library of Congress Cataloging-in-Publication Data
Names: Schulz, Erin Frances, (1975-) author
Title: Super Doll
Description: New Bedford: W.S. Beetle & Co., 2019

Identifiers:
LCCN: 2019918273
ISBN 978.0.9791783.7.5 (Hardcover)
ISBN 978.0.9791783.68 (Paperback)
ISBN 978.09791783.82 (eBook)

Cover design © Janet Schulz
www.superdollthenovel.com

PRAISE FOR "SUPER DOLL"

READER'S FAVORITE BOOK AWARD
FINALIST: YOUNG ADULT THRILLER

Author Erin Schulz tells a culturally unique and fascinatingly realistic tale of magic, romance, and independence that young adult readers are sure to enjoy, and adult readers will find much to adore too.

- 5 Stars, K.C. Finn for Readers' Favorite

A hard-to-put-down story with a fascinating setting and memorable characters.

- 5 Stars, R. Dzemo for Readers' Favorite

Super Doll is an empowering and atmospheric read for teens who love prophecies, unexpected romances, and stories set in completely foreign countries!

- Goodreads Reviewer

There were twists and turns, making everything you think is going to happen NOT! If you love fantasy, this will be your new favorite read!

- Carly-Rae, Hey It's Carly-Rae! Book Club

To Milly

Who helped make this book possible

P.S. I got up at 7:02am Pacific Time

CONTENTS

An Island Missing From Maps

Our little airplane bursts through the cloud bank into the sun, conquering in a nanosecond the turbulence that has plagued us since takeoff. My window shade is open, and I'm accosted by the sudden change of light. *Severe clear*. An Air Force term from my dad's world.

Even though I'm seated in the last row, the solitary flight attendant rather thoughtfully serves me first. On the linen-covered tray rests an egg salad sandwich and a tiny piece of chocolate cake. It has been hours since my last meal, but I slide the tray table away from me and slump lower in my seat. I can't think about eating.

Not now.

Not after what happened.

"Are you okay, honey?" the flight attendant asks. She looks crisp and neat, her dark uniform pressed and tailored to her frame.

"The hurricane," I murmur. I don't know how else to explain my disheveled appearance. My clothes are soaked and tattered. My hair is a tangled, windblown mess.

She either misunderstands me or is being kind. Her smile, it is sympathetic. "Oh, don't worry," she says. "We're flying far ahead of it now. Your island will be fine, I'm sure." She pats my shoulder and moves on.

My island?

Was it ever mine? Could it still be?

With Julian, perhaps.

I clutch the black velvet pouch tighter in my palm. I think of the journal I left behind covered in black lace by Becky with love. Black velvet and black lace. Black sugar and black diamonds. Storm clouds over an island gone astray, an island missing from maps.

How did it all begin? One second I was an ordinary military brat, dreaming big. "Dreaming of prairies without fences," my dad once said. The next second, I was somebody. But who? The girlfriend of an uncrowned prince? The doppelganger of a dead island queen. Or, alarmingly, someone much, much more.

THIS SAGA STARTED ON WHAT SHOULD HAVE BEEN A forgettable Thursday in May. Had the fire alarm not gone off in the middle of calculus, and had Mr. Carlton not accidentally locked the classroom door behind us when we evacuated and promptly lost his keys, I never would have seen the advertisement for the essay contest.

I never would have gone to the island. I never would have met Coco or Orchid. Or Julian.

Especially Julian.

The advertisement was thumbtacked to one of those bulletin boards no one ever looks at, and I wouldn't have, either, except we were stuck in the hall-way, waiting for Carlton to find a spare set of keys. For lack of anything better to do, I stifled a yawn and stared at the bulletin board. It was filled with club announce-ments on colored paper, all stamped with smiley faces and the words "Approved by the Administration."

What caught my attention was a photograph near the top of the board. Next to a massive promotion for class rings was a picture of a beautiful place. Triangular, dark-green mountains draped by clouds. An aquamarine sea washing up on a beach lined with palms.

This Summer Learn Spanish Through the Immersion Method, the poster read in black letters. It was followed by a tempting invitation. *Essay Contest: Win the Chance to Spend Eight Weeks on the Caribbean island of Carabajel with the Intercultural Language Institute*.

There were little serrated tabs at the bottom of the poster with the contest information. It sounded pretty simple. I had to write one thousand words on how language unites the world and email it to the address listed on the tab. I knew it was a long shot at best. But I really did need to learn Spanish. And fast.

Two months before, I had received word I'd been accepted into the international studies program at Vassar College on one nearly impossible condition—I needed to arrive on campus in September with fluency in the language of my choice. Not an easy feat considering even though I was in Advanced Placement Spanish, my conversation skills were borderline non-existent.

I tore off one of the tabs and put it in my pocket when I thought no one was looking.

"Spanish, huh?" I jumped at the noise and turned to see one of the varsity baseball players standing over me. His name was either Ted or T.J.

"I saw you got into Vassar, Pipes," he said. "I always knew you were a smart cookie."

"Yes," I replied, "and I heard you got into..." I let my voice trail off because I actually had no idea where he had been accepted. Sandy Point High School prided itself on being college prep, and the guidance department put up a huge congratulatory poster in the main lobby with everyone's name and college. But I wasn't sure what this guy's first name was, let alone his last name.

The one thing no one ever tells you about being an Air Force kid and moving around from place to place is people start to look the same. Not sort of the same, but exactly the same. Marlene from Austin looks exactly like Elizabeth from Albuquerque, and Tara looks even more like Jackie from Cheyenne. Chris resembles Angelo, and Angelo is a dead ringer for Adam. And if there is one thing in this life that will kill a possible friendship immediately, it's repeatedly calling someone the wrong name. I always tried to be a part of my class and fit in, but sometimes it was too hard to keep track of whether it was Tara/Jackie who stole Adam/Angelo, or if I was remembering that from another school.

Meanwhile, Ted/T.J. was still grinning down at me. "I got accepted to Stevens Tech," he said. "It's still Jersey, but I'm going to party it up in Hoboken. You around for the summer?"

I nodded. "I don't leave until late August."

And I was counting down the days. As far as I was concerned, Vassar was a ticket out of the dull towns and military bases that defined my life. I was dead tired of the regimented lifestyle, the gray buildings, and the talk of desert wars. I wanted exoticism instead of drabness. I wanted to see places where everything didn't match, places unlike our duplex housing units with officers drifting about in identical uniforms.

In my seventeen years, we had lived on six bases in six states—Alaska, Nevada, Texas, Wyoming, New

Mexico, and New Jersey—and each one was nearly indistinguishable from the others. To tranquilize myself against the sterility, I collected old maps, read travel blogs, and stared at my nightlight globe, plotting the day when I would escape the Air Force.

Someone at the end of the hallway of lockers yelled, "Richardson, let's go!" and Ted/T.J. hollered, "Yeah, man!"

Before he headed off in the direction of his friend, he said, "Text me this summer, Pipes. We can hang out or something."

"Yes, or something," I replied, somewhat surprised. I didn't get many invitations.

In the eight months we had been stationed on Sandy Point, I had managed to make all of about two friends and three acquaintances. I wasn't against anyone, and no one was against me. I just didn't make much of an effort considering it was already senior year. I was also kind of obsessed with studying. I realized early on a high grade point average was the key to my future. Needless to say, I spent a lot of weekends hanging around the house with my father and his new wife, Becky.

For the rest of the day, I thought about the essay contest and how random it would be if I actually won. I didn't think I had a fighting chance. I never had exceptionally good luck. But later, after dinner, I was a little excited when I took the tab out of my pocket and turned on my laptop.

I wrote about my Finnish mother who came to America when she married my father. She died from mental illness because she couldn't express the pain of her existence on the isolated Alaskan base with her limited English. I wrote about how I barely remembered her, but I knew from photographs she bequeathed me her face and her white-blonde hair even though she didn't wear it in dreadlocks like me. I argued had she learned English properly through instruction rather than half-hearted attempts to pick it up from television, she might have been better able to communicate the extent of the demons that haunted her. I wasn't sure I was writing the entire truth, but every so often, my dad lamented the inadequacy of the base hospital and his own inadequacy for not recognizing the warning signs of suicide.

She hid behind an extraordinary reserve, I typed, *or so my father says. Language could have saved her life.*

A few weeks later, a congratulatory letter from the Institute arrived the old-fashioned way—in our mailbox. I stood frozen in place, astonished I had actually pulled it off. Instead of spending the summer on base with a language tutor, I would be living on an island in the Caribbean Sea.

I didn't know if I should laugh, cry, or jump for joy. First Vassar, then the contest. It was beyond belief.

I read the letter twice to be sure I had not missed anything. I couldn't fathom it really said, *Dear Ruth Pfeiffer, we are delighted to inform you...*

It went on to explain, in a fashion a little too brief for my liking, that for decades the island of Carabajel had been closed to tourism, and its only communication with the outside world was based entirely on the exportation of a rare black sugar. Only recently had Carabajel's military regime started to move the island out of its self-inflicted isolation.

The Institute noted my acceptance would grant me unprecedented access to an island shrouded in mystery. They used words like adventure, exploration, and intercultural communication. They said it was my chance to be a true ambassador of the United States, along with the seven other high school graduates who had signed up for the program.

Once I was confident I was not dreaming, it occurred to me for all my love of geography, I knew absolutely nothing about where I was going. I raced up to my room and turned on my laptop.

At first, the online map registered the island as a tiny speck in the blue Caribbean Sea, due north of Colombia. But when I zoomed in to try to get a closer look, the detail of the island refused to load. Even the satellite view displayed nothing more than a green blob.

Undeterred, mostly out of fear of telling my dad I

was going to spend the summer on an island I knew absolutely nothing about, I opened up my browser and searched Carabajel.

But the Internet was little help. It described the island as remote, impenetrable, and mystical—a place cut off by reefs and drenched in fog, its surrounding waters littered with the wreckage of downed ships and planes. A mid-century navigator was even quoted a bit disconcertingly as saying it was a land of sacrilege. The few photographs I managed to find showed a paradise of lush beauty just like the essay contest poster. The sharp, triangular mountains. The palm trees lining the banks of a black sand beach. A city hidden by mist.

"Of all places!" my dad exclaimed when he heard the news. We were having dinner at the Officers' Club where we ate every Friday night. He was wavering between being thrilled I won an essay contest and being deliriously unhappy I was leaving home sooner than August.

Becky, however, said, "Piper, how fantastic."

"It is fantastic she won, yes, but heck, she can learn a language here without flying off to some deserted island." He slapped the table with his palm for emphasis.

"It's more than learning a language, Dad. I'm going to be an intercultural ambassador."

"And what exactly does that mean?"

Becky jumped in to save me. "Steve, she beat out hundreds of other applicants to win this contest. The Intercultural Language Institute is very prestigious. This is an honor, indeed."

My father looked skeptical, and I was shocked Becky had even heard of the program. Unless she just pretended to know it to help me. Before my father could get back to his original question about what I would be doing in my role as an ambassador, I blurted out the concrete details. "I will be gone from June 17th to August 17th, and everything is paid for—my flight, accommodations, meals—everything."

The fact all the costs were covered by the program pacified my father a bit. It is no secret the budgets of military men are always a little tight. I conveniently left out the tiny detail about the Institute suggesting I bring a small amount of spending money, but I wasn't too concerned. I had a little saved up from working afternoons and weekends at the library on base. Besides, I couldn't imagine what I would need to spend my money on, considering I was going to an isolated island in the middle of the sea.

"Also, Dad," I added, "at the end of the program, I'll be able to take the language requirement exam at Vassar."

"This will count at Vassar?" he asked.

I nodded.

My father shook his head with resignation. "I'm not

sure why we are even discussing this, Piper, because you are going to do what you want to do anyway."

"You make it sound like I'm rebelling, but I swear, I'm not," I protested.

"That's a first," he said sounding annoyed. But he was smiling.

When we got home from dinner, I signed the acceptance letter and dropped it in the mailbox on the corner. Then I took Arthur, my Shiba Inu, to the abandoned stretch of beach by the old fort. I sat down on the sand and leaned back on my elbows while Arthur ran in circles, chasing seagulls.

Way off in the distance, I could see the skyscrapers of Manhattan and the parachute jump on Coney Island. I watched as a jumbo jet took off from JFK airport and headed east above the anchored freighters in the channel. The thought that I would soon be on a plane lifting off for somewhere filled me with a rush of excitement. The seventeenth of June was less than a month away. I had little to do except finish my senior year, graduate, and apologize to my boss at the base library for bailing on her for the summer.

I stayed on the beach long after dusk and waited for the stars even though I never could quite see them on Sandy Point. Not like the way I used to out west.

"The glow of the city lights obscures the night sky," the speaker at the base planetarium once told our class.

"Go offshore, and the stars will fall around you as though you are in a snow globe made of diamonds."

A snow globe made of diamonds.

Black sugar and black diamonds. Black velvet and black lace.

How ignorant I had been then to worlds beyond my own.

Welcome to Carabajel

On the day of my departure, my dad and Becky drove me to Newark Airport in our SUV. I put my two bags on the back seat so Arthur could come along and ride in the hatchback. I didn't have anyone else to say goodbye to. My dad offered to throw me a going-away party, but I settled for a lobster roll dinner at the Humpty Dumpty, my favorite restaurant on the shore.

"What airline are you flying?" my dad asked for the tenth time. We pulled off the New Jersey Turnpike, and the billboards matching airlines to terminals were fast approaching.

"American," I said again. "I am flying American Airlines, then Carabajel Air to the island." He didn't know I had two plane changes ahead of me. I also hadn't mentioned Carabajel Air—the only way to access the island—had just one flight per day, so if American was delayed into Costa Rica, I would have to spend the next twenty-four hours in the San Jose airport.

My dad swerved to the right as he tried to read the first sign, and a taxi driver alongside us slammed on his horn.

"Are you nervous?" Becky asked. She turned in her seat with a cheery smile plastered on her face.

I thought about what I was about to do—head out at age seventeen to spend eight weeks on an island I was ninety-nine percent certain had no Internet and only fifty percent certain had electricity.

"Nervous? Ah, no," I lied.

When we pulled up to the departures curb, I reached over the back seat to put my arms around Arthur's neck and he licked my face. Cars piled up behind us, but my dad and Becky stepped out of the SUV anyway and hugged me. Becky handed me the writing journal she had wrapped with black lace.

"Now you have a scrapbook too," she said. "You can record everything about your trip."

I grinned. "Thanks, Becky. I totally love it."

When my dad first brought her around, I couldn't believe they had anything in common. She told me her favorite hobby was scrapbooking, and I had no idea what she was talking about. She was pretty enough, but nothing at all like my dad. She had completed an alternative medicine program, grew things like wheatgrass, and didn't believe in pasteurizing milk. I didn't think she would last very long with my straitlaced dad until I caught him once chewing on a handful of greens to ward off a cold.

I pulled my backpack on and turned to my dad. "I'll call you as soon as I can."

"Ridiculous not to have email," my dad said. Again.

"They said there probably won't be Internet. *Probably*. Which means there could be. And there will be phones and the post office."

"It's going to be an adventure," Becky chirped. She pinched my dad's arm. "It's the cultural chance of a lifetime."

My dad looked at Becky and then back at me and threw up his hands. "Be careful, kid. And if you have any problems, offer bribes."

"Steven!" Becky exclaimed. "Piper, you just be your sweet self, and doors will open for you."

Other cars started blowing their horns, and an airport security guard in a white car put his flashing lights on, signaling my dad to move the SUV. I breathed a sigh of relief. He didn't have time to start another tirade about the island's lack of telecommunications.

I waved goodbye as they drove off, and I only got teary for a second when I saw Arthur turn around and put his front paws on the rear window. He watched me until a hotel shuttle bus pulled behind them and blocked his view.

Inside the airport, I bought a chocolate chip muffin at one of the breakfast cafés and found a place to sit by the window so I could watch the planes. I dug my favorite purple pen out of my purse and opened the lace journal. On the first page, I wrote down the date and underlined it, but I was at a loss for words as to what to write next. I was too excited about what was ahead of me. I closed the journal and took the itinerary from the Institute out of my backpack, even though I had read it at least ten times already.

I was scheduled to fly from Newark to Miami where I had to change planes for San Jose, Costa Rica. From there, I would board the Carabajel Air flight to the island. When I landed in Carabajel, a driver from the Institute would be waiting for me outside the terminal to bring me to my dorm. The program was taking place at Carabajel's only college.

At exactly quarter to nine, my plane took off into the sun. We circled once after takeoff for no apparent reason, but I was glad we did because I got to see our Air Force base and the long line of officers' homes stretching along the spit of land at Sandy Point.

In Miami, I ran through an endless maze of a terminal to get to my next gate. My flight was on final boarding when I raced up to the jet bridge, panting and cursing myself for sharing cigarettes all spring with Jamie, my fellow bookshelf stocker at the library.

The entire plane was filled with a group of Americans going on a golf tour. They were all wearing matching tournament shirts and talking about how easy it was to find a decent prime rib in Costa Rica.

The flight was totally uneventful, except for listening to the hum of the golfers talking about nine holes and eighteen holes and wind handicaps. When we finally landed in Costa Rica, an airport official in a white shirt directed me and the few other passengers connecting to Carabajel to take a shuttle bus from the main terminal to a rather decrepit, round building across the runway. Its brass door handles were tarnished, and the window boxes were filled with overgrown weeds. There were a few rusted prop planes parked nearby, their wheels chained to cement blocks set into the high grass.

We stood on the tarmac, waiting under the late afternoon sun. It was sweltering. Whatever sense of adventure I had when I left Newark was slowly being deflated by the merciless temperature. I huddled in a tiny patch of shade near the building, but next to me, the wheels of my suitcase were sinking into the melting asphalt.

For over an hour, I scanned the sky for the Carabajel Air plane with the other bedraggled travelers. When the plane finally did arrive, it was an alarming sight. The thing was old, very old. I stood there horrified, watching it sway out of the clouds, the silver fuselage glinting in the sun. It landed and came to a stop a hundred yards away from us, resting on a little tail wheel, its nose pointed skyward as though searching for the air.

"Is that our plane?" a woman shrieked. No one answered her. No one had to. "Carabajel Air" was painted on the plane's side in huge, slightly uneven blue letters.

A young, dark-haired pilot wearing aviator sunglasses lowered the door in the rear and stepped out of it with a clipboard. He beckoned for us to come forward, so we dragged our luggage toward him in silence. We handed him our boarding passes as we mounted the steps and had to almost climb vertically to our seats. I was assigned a window seat near the front, next to a man sweating profusely in his blue suit jacket.

Once everyone was aboard, the pilot made an announcement in Spanish and slammed the cockpit door shut behind him. The engines coughed to life before clamoring to a full roar. When it came time to take off, I squeezed my eyes shut. I wasn't usually afraid to fly. I'd been flying with my dad my whole life, but this particular airplane was exceeding the limits of my bravery. I tried to block from my memory everything I'd read about planes crashing in attempts to find Carabajel.

The flight was turbulent. But much to my surprise, perhaps because of the heat, I got accustomed to the bumpy air and found I was being lulled to sleep. I only woke up when I felt the nose of the plane slant downward at an angle that couldn't possibly be safe. My hands gripped the armrests, and I leaned over to look out the window. Nighttime had descended around us, yet even in the darkness, I could tell we had flown into a thundercloud. Raindrops pelted the window and rushed backward in long, narrow streaks.

Moments later, the pilot came over the intercom and made an eerily calm announcement in Spanish and then somewhat broken English that we should fasten our seatbelts for landing. The engines were alternately slowing down and speeding up, and in between, the whole plane was dropping, taking my stomach with it. Something metallic crashed to the floor in the back, and the man sitting next to me sat up straighter in his seat and said, "Maybe this is why no one leaves."

I turned to look at him, and he smiled a little and shrugged at the same time. "That's what they say, anyway. You must have heard?"

I shook my head. "I'm sorry, no."

"There is supposedly a myth about the island being so beautiful, it traps you there. I think it is rather because no one ever wants to board this plane again."

I was about to ask him where he heard the myth, but the plane dropped lower and the right wing dipped so sharply the window was almost underneath me. I grabbed the armrests again and took a deep breath, valiantly trying to rally my courage. We endured another big drop before there was a feeling of utter serenity.

I was surprised to see we were much lower than I had expected. We had broken through the cloudbank, and we were flying over water past a small mountain range. The moon wasn't full, but it was bright enough to see the ripples in the sea beneath us. The plane was clinging to the edge of the island and tiny lights, which I assumed were houses, dotted the mountainside.

I pressed my nose against the window and craned my neck to try to get a better look. Up ahead a rotating beacon and two high spotlights glowed on the edge of the shore. Below them were the dotted blue lights that marked the runway. The pilot eased the plane lower and lower until I could even see whitecaps forming on the tips of the waves. Suddenly, there was a surge of breakneck speed and the jolt of the wheels touching the runway. We rushed forward, brakes squealing. A second later, the plane came to a dead stop and the engines cut out.

Some of the other passengers started clapping, but my hands were still glued to the armrests. The cockpit door flew open and the pilot stepped into the aisle. "Bienvenida to Carabajel," he said as he walked past our seats.

"I'm impressed," the man next to me commented. "And I'm a pilot." He stood up and opened the overhead bin.

I unfastened my seatbelt and pulled my backpack out from under the seat in front of me. I reread the arrival instructions one more time. *Proceed toward the terminal after collecting your luggage. Go through customs, and outside the main door a representative will be waiting for you with a sign for the Intercultural Language Institute. He will bring you to your dormitory for check-in.*

I waited until the other passengers deplaned, and then I pulled up the hood of my sweatshirt to cover my now-tangled dreadlocks. I held on to the other seats as I stumbled down the aisle toward the door in the tail. The moment my foot touched the jet stairs, I was hit by a wall of smoldering, fragrant air. I stopped on the top step and inhaled deeply. It was intoxicating, as though I'd stepped into a garden hothouse filled with lilies and...cookies? I couldn't place the scent.

A ground crew member was waiting at the bottom of the steps, beckoning for me to come down.

"Last?" he asked.

"Yes," I replied.

He pointed to my suitcase, which was sitting all by itself next to the plane, and then to the green stucco terminal. The rest of the passengers from my flight had already crossed the tarmac and were straggling through the terminal door.

I walked down the air steps and picked up my bag. The terminal in front of me was a tiny rectangular building with a glass control tower on the roof. There were palm trees everywhere, and hibiscus plants dripped down the side of the building like ivy. As I followed everyone else, I passed a small round fountain filled with tiny goldfish glittering in the underwater lights. I was about to open the glass door to the terminal when I stopped and turned around.

I looked at the fountain again. I glanced back toward the end of the runway where the death trap of a plane was sitting. There was something about the entire scene I could not quite put my finger on. I took a few steps forward and reached out to touch the edge of the fountain.

It was impossible. Utterly impossible.

But I had an overwhelming sense I had seen that fountain before.

The Night Carnival

I pushed the terminal's glass door open and stepped into a room painted a shade resembling pistachio ice cream. Faded but polished linoleum covered the entire floor.

Customs was more rigid than I expected for a tiny Caribbean island. An imposing man in a black uniform with gold lapels looked taken aback when I approached his desk. He eyed me and my luggage for a long moment before speaking.

"What did you bring with you from beyond our shores?" he asked in a booming voice.

It was a strange question. "Um, nothing. Clothes, I guess," I replied.

"We have strict regulations on Carabajel." He

gestured behind him at a poster with images of items banned by the island's authorities. There were some obvious ones—plants, guns, and fireworks—but also comic books, a stack of brochures, an ancient radio, an even older looking camera, and something that must have been a Vietnam War-era portable phone.

I shook my head. "I can safely say I'm not carrying any of those items."

My tone must have been too much because he gestured to another official and then to my luggage. The other official hoisted my suitcase up and put it on the table while the original officer scrutinized my passport and the little customs document I had filled out on the plane. I regretted the two packages of peanut butter cookies I had squirreled away under my pajamas.

"What is the purpose of your travel here?" the first officer asked.

"I'm a student with the Intercultural Language Institute."

He jumped in surprise. "Halt!" he yelled at the man who was about to unzip my suitcase. "You did not say so, Miss—" he looked down at my papers— "Miss Pfeiffer."

I bit my tongue before I told him he hadn't exactly given me the chance. My suitcase went back on the ground with a broad smile. A large stamp came out, and an ink mark with the initials "GMC" inside an oval crest was stamped in my passport. I already knew from my somewhat futile Internet search that the initials stood for the leader of the island, General Miguel Castillo.

"We here on Carabajel welcome you and all of the Intercultural Language Institute students," the officer said. "You are a sign of a great many things to come for our island."

"Thank you," I muttered as I wheeled my luggage away, relieved to be out of customs with my stash of cookies intact.

I headed toward the exit doors. Through the glass window, I saw a giant tree near a rotary across the street. Its branches were craggy and gnarled, and the root system spilled out over the top of the ground. The unnerving feeling that I had at the fountain hit me again, and my breath caught in my chest. I pictured small white objects lined up in rows.

I cupped my hands around my face and stared through the glass, squinting to see beyond the room's reflection. "A cemetery?" I whispered. The sound of my own voice jolted me to my senses. *You are losing it, Piper. Get a grip.*

I forced myself to keep walking toward the main exit. When I pushed open the door, the rush of sugar-sweet air hit me again. I closed my eyes and took a deep breath. It took all of my willpower to open my eyes again and look at the tree. I peered into the darkness, the moon illuminating an arc around the tree and the field beyond it. But the field was empty. There was no cemetery in sight. A nervous, relieved laugh erupted from my mouth.

Shaking off the cemetery incident, I proceeded to the area where the Institute driver was supposedly waiting. A battered orange cab pulled up alongside me. The driver leaned out the window. "Ride, señorita?" he asked.

"No, I'm all set, thank you. I have a ride."

"There are only two taxis in Carabajel! If I leave, you have no one. All alone! No one to get you!"

I was sure he meant well, but his tone made me cringe. "I have a ride, thanks," I repeated. The driver shrugged and drove off in a cloud of dust.

The airport parking lot was empty, but the taxi stand was massive, especially if it was only for two taxis. Ahead of me at the end of the block, a small multi-colored bus was waiting. Crossing my fingers it was the Institute driver, I picked up my pace.

When I got closer, a man stepped out of the bus. "Señorita Pfeiffer? Intercultural Language Institute?"

I sighed with relief. "Yes and yes."

"Bienvenida to Carabajel," he said.

As he took my suitcase, I got a closer look at the vehicle. It was odd. The front part was shaped like a truck, but the back had been turned into an open tour bus with bench seats and a canvas roof.

I was clearly the only person the driver was waiting

for because once I was seated, he started the engine and put the bus in gear. We headed down the airport driveway to a road that ran along the edge of the sea. The moment I leaned back on the bench seat, I began to feel tired. I sank lower in my seat and fought the urge to drift off. Even though I was exhausted, the moonlight was brighter than it had been on the airplane, so I tried my best to take in the island as we drove.

Carabajel was more breathtaking than it had looked in the photographs. The mountains rising up above a crescent-shaped beach were the same ones from the essay contest poster. There were palm trees and black-lavender flowers everywhere. They looked like they belonged in a manicured botanical garden. I watched the scenery as long as I could before I wedged my back-pack behind my neck and rested my head against it.

The next thing I knew, I swore I heard a voice call me by my never-used first name. "Ruth?"

I sat up to look at the driver, but he was staring straight ahead at the road. Thinking he had tried to wake me, I said, "I'm sorry. Are we there?"

"No, no." He shook his head. "Pronto. Carabajel City first."

The bus turned sharply, and my backpack slid to the floor. I leaned over to retrieve it. When I looked up again, I gasped in amazement.

We were entering a walled downtown. The massive stone wall stretched as far to the left and right as I could see in the darkness. The driver proceeded slowly through an archway supported by carved statues. One of the statue's hands held up the base of the arch. The other statue's hand was extended and held a gaslight with a tremendous flame.

I was so fascinated by my surroundings I couldn't help but ask the driver to slow down. "Reducir la velocidad, por favor?" I asked, pleased with myself for speaking Spanish.

The driver downshifted the bus to a crawl. I leaned over the edge to gape at the statues as we drove through the arch. It was hard to tell if they were granite or marble, but they clearly depicted beautiful women staring fiercely at each other. The most peculiar thing about them was their garb. Instead of the usual scantily clad statues you see in museums, these women were covered from head to toe in carved fabric.

As soon as we were through the archway, the driver picked up speed again, but only enough to keep us moving, since the pavement had turned to cobblestones and the bus was rattling about significantly. I stared at Carabajel City in awe. Gaslights burned at every corner, bathing the sandstone buildings on the street in an unsettling glow. All the shops and cafés had candles in their darkened windows. I imagined how vibrant the scene would be in the daylight. It wouldn't look anything like New Jersey, that was for sure.

The driver turned down a narrow road and stopped

short. We had driven right into a carnival of sorts. Street vendors lined the sidewalks while men in dark clothes and women wearing filmy gowns drifted amongst them. Some held lanterns and candles, and others were ringing handbells, but all of them chanted a low, mesmerizing song. Something was peculiar about the scene, though. It took me a moment to figure out that while it looked like a carnival, no one appeared particularly happy. Every person we passed looked somber, and the music sounded more like a death march than a celebration.

I leaned forward so the driver could hear me. "Excuse me. What is all of this?" I asked.

He looked at me in the rearview mirror as we inched along, and I gestured around us. He paused before saying something in Spanish I didn't understand.

"Carnaval?" I asked.

"No, no carnaval. Religiosa."

"It's a religious celebration?" I asked.

The driver shook his head. "No es una celebracion."

I gave up and leaned back in my seat. I tried not to make eye contact with anyone on the street because I felt as though I had crashed a private party. Part of me wished the driver would go faster, but the other part of me was mesmerized by the scene unfolding around me.

The women in particular were enchanting. Their gowns looked like they were made of smoke—like if you grasped the fabric it would disappear. But it was their faces that were truly extraordinary. Even the older women had high cheekbones and long, dark hair, and some of them wore veils running down the length of their bodies to touch the ground. As intriguing as it was, I still breathed a sigh of relief when we finally drove away from the gathering.

The Universidad de Villegas was on the other side of the wall less than a mile from the city. When we finally pulled into the driveway, the place reminded me of a hotel from another era, not a college campus. Three-story octagon buildings were connected by little paths through immense gardens and palm trees. A barrier of thick mangroves lined the embankment on the property line. Almost all of the buildings stood dark except for a low glass one with a carport situated near the edge of the seawall.

The driver pulled up in front of it and stopped the bus. I pushed my hoodie down and tried to smooth my dreadlocks. The driver turned to me and opened his mouth to speak, but then suddenly reeled back around to face the windshield.

"Thank you very much," I said as I hopped down. It occurred to me I was probably supposed to tip him, so I started sifting through my backpack for my wallet. I had just curled my fingers around it when he came up behind me and practically threw my suitcase onto the curb. A second later, he was behind the wheel again zooming toward the road.

"Or maybe I'm not supposed to tip him," I said aloud. I had no idea what his problem was. He'd seemed nice enough when he picked me up. But I didn't want to waste too much time pondering it. Not when I still had to confront the lobby door. I was a little apprehensive in a first-day-at-a-new-school sort of way. I wanted to get it over with, but the door felt like it was made of lead.

The lobby resembled an outdated men's smoking lounge with wood paneled walls and a red-carpeted floor. A gray-haired woman in a light blue housekeeper's uniform sat behind a desk at the far end of the room engrossed in a book.

"Hi, I'm Ruth Pfeiffer," I said. She looked up and sprung out of her chair. Her book hit the floor and almost took her water glass with it on the way down.

I reached for her overturned book, but she beat me to it. She straightened up and stared at me wide-eyed, clutching her book to her chest.

"I'm so sorry I scared you," I said. "My name is Ruth Pfeiffer. I'm checking in?" It came out like a question and she narrowed her eyes.

I wondered if I was in the wrong place. But the other buildings had all been dark.

A female voice rescued me. From somewhere in the lobby, a sickeningly sweet inflection called out, "Hello, love, you're finally here."

I turned to see a glamorous girl with long brown

hair standing by the door. She was wearing a teeny skirt and high heels. She sauntered over to me and kissed me on both cheeks.

"Why didn't you fly with the rest of us yesterday?" she asked.

"I don't know," I replied. "Someone at the Institute booked my flights."

"Oh well, no matter. Now we are eight. I'm Aisling from New York City."

"I'm Piper."

"Where are you from?"

"I'm not really from anywhere."

She tilted her head. "What do you mean?"

"My dad's in the Air Force. We move around a lot."

"How super patriotic. I'm off to Yale in the fall. What about you?"

"Vassar."

"Lucky, but I was so hoping for another Yale girl." She looked around the lobby and frowned. "Where's my bag?" she asked.

"Your bag?"

"One of my bags got stuck in Costa Rica and was supposed to be on your flight. Didn't your driver bring it?"

"I don't think so," I replied. "I didn't see it. He didn't say anything to me."

"Unbelievable!" Aisling put her hands on her hips

and looked over my shoulder. "Pilar, can you please help me? The driver didn't have my bag."

I looked back at the terrified check-in clerk. She was standing as erect as a soldier, her chin elevated, and her gaze fixed at something on the ceiling. She looked from Aisling to me and back to Aisling again.

"Si, yes. Un momento."

She shoved a form across the desk in my direction and indicated with a pen where I needed to sign. I scrawled my name at the bottom without reading it. Aisling slumped down on a couch by the door and looked at her phone.

"We have service here?" I asked.

"I wish. No bars, no signal, no roaming. Nothing. Even the old pay phone is broken." She nodded in the direction of a time-worn black phone mounted on the far wall.

"I'm really sorry about your bag," I said. "I had no idea."

"Not your fault, love." She shrugged and eyed my dreads. "Random cool hair," she added and looked back down at her phone. I wasn't sure if she had complimented me or criticized me—or both—so I said, "Thanks," and smiled at her.

"See you mañana. I'm in Room 327 if you need anything." She bounced off the couch and vanished through the lobby door.

I turned back to Pilar. I needed a room number and

a key. Or just a key with a room number on it. Either way, I wanted out of the lobby.

"You will come with me?" Pilar asked. She reached for my suitcase.

"I've got it," I said, waving her off. "Happy to carry it myself."

Pilar seemed skeptical, but she beckoned for me to follow her. We walked outside and up an open staircase built into the edge of the farthest octagon building. She led me to the third floor, unlocked the door to room 317, and gave me the key.

"Gracias," I said, but she had already pulled the door closed behind her, leaving me alone.

I paused in the small foyer of the room, marveling that everything before me was totally mine and mine alone for eight full weeks. I had never had such privacy or such space. To think, my own bathroom. Our military housing units were always sparse. They were attached, mirror-image duplexes with carports on the side, tiny bedrooms, and one shared bath. This room was huge in comparison, larger than most of our dining rooms. It had two twin beds pushed together, a writing desk and chair, a dresser, an overstuffed armchair, and a balcony with two café chairs and a little round table. The furnishings were worn, and the carpet was thread-bare, but I could have cared less.

I put my suitcase on the bed and opened the sliding balcony door. The fragrant air rushed in, but this time it was mixed with salty spray from the sea. My balcony overlooked what appeared to be a saltwater pool carved into the seawall. Beyond it was nothing but the blackness of the empty ocean.

I went back inside, pulling only the screen door shut behind me. The air in the room was stuffy, but I knew it would ventilate in no time with the door open. There was an air-conditioning unit in the corner, but air conditioning always gave me sinus problems, so I didn't turn it on.

I sat down on the bed and was momentarily at a loss as to what to do with myself. I wished I could call my dad, but as I suspected and Aisling confirmed, the phones were out.

I looked around again and spotted a small hand-written note on the night table underneath a paperweight in the shape of a sailfish.

Dear Ruth,

We are so happy you have joined us. Welcome to Carabajel. Tomorrow, breakfast will be served at 8am in the lobby, and class begins at 9am in the Reef Room. See you then!

Cecilia—Your ILI Instructor.

I looked at my watch. It was inching closer to midnight. I was so exhausted, I felt like I could sleep for days, but I decided on a hot shower first. The pipes in the bathroom creaked and groaned, but the water was gloriously warm.

After my shower, I pulled on an oversized tee shirt

and lay in bed, staring at the ceiling and listening to the ocean waves hitting the seawall. When sleep began to overtake me, I pulled the covers up to my ears and let myself drift off.

I don't know how long I was asleep, but I woke up with a start, gripped by the terror of a nightmare. I sat up straight and clumsily reached for the lamp next to the bed. I looked around frantically, but nothing had changed except for the balcony door curtains, which were now billowing like angry clouds. Even though I wanted the fresh air, the curtains were creeping me out, so I got up and slid the glass door shut.

When I climbed back into bed, I left the light on and tried for a long time to recall the nightmare. But it was gone.

❦ 4 ❦

The Nun on the Beach

I woke up to bright morning sun peeking in from behind the curtains and the digital clock by my bedside blinking 9:07 a.m. I pushed the covers off me and jumped up. Thanks to my nightmare and being awake until almost dawn, I totally overslept. I couldn't believe that with all my military training, I was exactly seven minutes late for class on my first day. I'd always been on a regimented schedule, courtesy of my dad. Twenty-four hours away from him, and apparently all that had gone out the window.

Taking a shower or having breakfast were no longer options, much to the chagrin of my tummy, which was now in total starvation mode. Adding to my frustration was the fact that I would be walking into a classroom filled with students who had already spent the previous two days getting to know one another.

When I finally made it downstairs, and into the Reef Room, everyone turned to stare at me. I met their gazes and immediately knew what the problem was. I had thrown on black shorts and a tank top, but compared to the way everyone else was dressed, I looked like I was on my way to fix someone's truck. The other girls were dressed more or less in the same fashion as Aisling, with miniskirts or flowery dresses and high heels.

The room itself was as unnerving as their stares. It had a turquoise carpet with red starfish everywhere, which made me feel like I was trapped on a coral reef. All of the windows were located against the far wall, and most of the chairs with tiny desks attached to them had been set up in a U-shape formation.

A lady with red hair wearing a paisley wrap skirt and a white tee shirt was standing at the front of the room behind a desk stacked with books. She looked up at me and said, "Ruth?"

"Sorry, jet lag," I murmured, which made no sense at all considering I hadn't changed time zones.

"It's okay," she said. "I'm Cecilia, your instructor. You missed the rest of the introductions, but I can go around the room and test my memory by telling you something about each student."

"Thanks," I said as I slid into a seat at the back of the room.

But Cecilia shook her head and motioned for me to move forward. "There are only eight of you, so you might as well all sit close together."

I groaned inwardly. I didn't feel like sitting so close to everyone, but I quickly reminded myself I was there on the Institute's dime because they picked my essay. Being late and ignoring Cecilia's instructions would probably get me a seat on the next flight back to Jersey.

I relocated to a chair between a girl named Sofia, who Cecilia introduced as the daughter of a former professional skier from Vail, and Gareth, the only guy in our class. In September, he was headed to Stanford to study environmental engineering. "For the third world," he leaned over and whispered to me.

Cecilia rattled off a few tidbits about the remaining five students, pausing every now and then so they could correct her. There was Coco, an Asian girl from Los Angeles who was so beautiful she looked as though she had stepped out of a cosmetics advertisement. And there was Bronwyn, a petite strawberry blonde from Connecticut who had already bonded with another girl named Gemma because they were both going to be freshmen at Smith. Gemma was from Long Island, New York. Her wrists were layered with gold bracelets, and on her right hand was a glass cocktail ring that matched her blue dress. Then there was Kimberlee from Mississippi, who was a tenth-generation Southerner and going to Ole Miss. And last was Aisling, the obvious cool girl of the class who I already knew was a slightly anorexic Manhattanite.

When Cecilia finished her monologue, she said it was my turn to stand up and introduce myself. I tried to speak loudly so no one would hear my stomach growling. My hunger had taken on an entirely new intensity.

"I'm Ruth Pfeiffer," I started, "but everyone calls me Piper. My father is in the Air Force, so I don't really have a home per se, but now we are living in New Jersey on the Sandy Point base and it's okay. I like being on the ocean. Oh, and I am starting the international studies program at Vassar in September."

As I started to sit back down in my chair, Cecilia said brightly, "And Ru—I mean Piper—is the recipient of our essay contest scholarship. She beat over three thousand other applicants to be here!" Cecilia started clapping and the class awkwardly followed her lead. I felt my face flush. The last thing I wanted was extra attention.

CONSIDERING ITS SOMEWHAT ROCKY START, THE morning passed quicker than I expected. When lunchtime came around, Cecilia dismissed us for an hour. A buffet table had been set up in the lobby, and I selected two pastries stuffed with pink guava jelly and a side of sliced mango, and then made a hasty exit outside. As usual, I felt like being alone.

The classroom had been chilly, and I wanted to warm up by the saltwater pool I had seen from my balcony. A light rain was falling even though it was sunny, but not enough to bother me. I headed for the edge of the property where the pool sat against the high seawall and plopped down in one of the lounge chairs.

When I finished my lunch, I looked at my watch. I still had more than enough time to explore a little before going back inside. I strolled over to the deep end and considered putting on my bathing suit so I could dive in but caught sight of a black sand beach below the seawall. I wondered how one got to it until I noticed a slightly overgrown footpath through the mangroves.

I followed the trail through the thicket and paused when I reached a small stream. It wasn't narrow enough for me to jump over it, so I kicked off my sandals and waded through the cool water, my feet making hollow suctions in the velvety sand. I put my sandals back on when I crossed to the other side, and I walked tentatively down a slippery hill until the beach came into view. Low-hanging palm trees and vines cast shadows on the water and made the sea look black and glossy like spilled ink.

I had never seen black sand before, so I bent down and picked up a handful of it. As I let it run through my fingers, a small purple-black stone remained in my palm. It was so clear, it almost looked like the sea glass I collected when I took Arthur for walks on the Jersey shore. I thought about pocketing it, but I decided to make a wish instead.

I stepped closer to the water and held the rock tightly between my fingers. I wanted something special for my stone, but I didn't know what to wish for. I opened my eyes anyway and threw it as far out as I could manage. Right before it hit the water, my wish came to me.

"I want to find where I belong," I whispered. It sounded like a cliché, but it was true. Ever since I got accepted to Vassar, I dreamed of my life changing. I wanted so desperately to find my place in the world.

My purple stone splashed down and broke the stillness of the water, leaving circular ripples in its wake. I watched the circles gradually grow larger until they turned into small round waves. I yawned and stretched my arms over my head. It was such a tranquil scene, I wished I could lie down on the sand and take a nap.

And then I saw her.

I drew in a sharp breath and almost screamed despite myself. Standing twenty feet away from me, on the edge of a little atoll, was a nun. She was dressed entirely in black and she was watching me, unmoving. A large diamond cross dangled from a choker around her neck, and her veil was mounted on the top of her head as though it were a crown. She looked eerily like the statues guarding the entrance to Carabajel City.

I wasn't sure if I should wave to her, say hello, or run for my life. Before I could decide, she stepped off the atoll and began to walk toward me ever so slowly. She strolled indifferently on the edge of the water, unconcerned that the sea was almost touching her shoes.

As she grew closer, I could smell a heavy, rich perfume. I was taken aback for a moment when I saw she was beautiful, perhaps even the most beautiful woman I had ever seen. Her cheekbones were high on her face, and the edge of her jaw was perfectly defined. Her eyebrows were arched over large violet eyes rimmed with kohl, and her lips were full and the palest shade of pink.

Suddenly she stopped short in her tracks and her eyes narrowed to slits. She looked at me closely before spinning around abruptly and walking in the opposite direction. She paused only once to look at the horizon. I followed her gaze, but there was nothing out there besides the endless sea. Without ever turning back to me, she continued on her way, her gown billowing behind her until she became just a speck in the distance.

Only then did I run.

I dashed back up the footpath and across the stream without even taking my sandals off. When I finally reached the saltwater pool, I collapsed into one of the lounge chairs and tried to catch my breath. As superficial a thought as it was, I couldn't help but wonder why on earth a woman so glamorous would have joined a convent. Then the thought occurred to me—perhaps she wasn't a nun after all. When we lived in New Mexico, there was a private Catholic school near our base. Sometimes I would see the nuns from the convent at the drugstore or the grocery store dressed in their full habits, even if the temperature was one hundred degrees. Those nuns certainly never wore makeup or diamonds.

I pulled the elastic out of my ponytail and let my dreadlocks free. I tried to shake the possible nun episode off my shoulders. I knew I was acting like a complete idiot, especially because the woman hadn't said one word to me. But it was her expression that had flustered me the most.

She had looked at me as though she recognized me.

I closed my eyes and tried to steady my nerves until the unmistakable sound of high heels on pavement came up behind my chair. I feared the nun had returned, so I was beyond happy when I looked up and saw it was only Coco, looking at me from behind heart-shaped white sunglasses.

"It's Fifi, no?" she asked.

"No, Piper," I corrected.

She looked confused for a second, but then reached over my head and opened the sun umbrella behind me.

"You don't mind, do you? The sun is murder on your skin."

I shrugged my shoulders, and she sat down next to me.

"You said you were going to Vassar, right?" she asked.

I shaded my eyes with my hand. "Yes, Vassar."

"I thought about applying there, but I want to go into fashion. You must have good grades," she added.

"I do okay."

"Like, what is okay, if you don't mind me asking?"

"Oh, um, like a 3.9."

"Wow," she said. "That's amazing. And your essays too."

"My Vassar essays?" I asked.

"Yes, those, and you won the scholarship for this program too, so you must be able to write a killer essay."

"I don't know. I think I got lucky."

Coco picked at something invisible on her glossy manicure. "You are definitely lucky. I try to write, but it takes me ages. Have you heard of the Prix de Paris?"

I shook my head.

"It is a fashion contest from the 1950s. Jackie Kennedy even won once. Well, this group of designers brought it back this year. And I want to win it."

"What do you win?"

"A whole year in Paris! Studying fashion of course."

"It must be competitive."

"It is. And my essay is awful. I know it is."

"What's the topic?"

"How haute couture is art."

"Oh," I said. I wasn't sure how else to respond. I had never thought to consider clothes as art.

"Why is a couture dress different from a painting?" she asked. "The handiwork is exquisite. It is a dying art."

"I really never thought about it that way," I admitted. I looked at her white dress with its tiny gold belt and her white patent leather high heels and felt shabby in comparison.

"Everyone defines art their own way," she continued. "To me, art is fashion. And your art is clearly something else." I must have made a face because she gasped. "I'm sorry, Piper. I didn't mean to sound offensive."

"No problem." She had a point. Fashion and I were never quite friends.

"I actually wanted to ask you something," she continued, her pretty face colored by the blue umbrella. "We are all stuck together for a while, so I was wondering if you would help me with my essay?"

She looked so hopeful, I felt myself nod. "But I'm not sure I'm the right person to help you. I don't know anything about fashion or even art."

Coco grinned a row of perfectly white teeth. "I'll

provide all the thoughts. I just need to get it on paper and make it sound brilliant. You'll really help?"

I nodded again. "I'll certainly try."

She stood up and squeezed my arm. "You are my new bestie!"

Coco slung her white purse onto her shoulder. "See you in a few. Oh, I almost forgot, we're all going into Carabajel City tonight. Do you want to come?"

I hesitated. "We'll see," I said. "I'm pretty exhausted, but thanks."

"You should totally come, but suit yourself," she replied. "We're meeting in the lobby at six o'clock."

The Pastry Shop

A few hours later, I was lying on my bed mindlessly drawing sketches of flowers in my journal when I heard voices in the hall outside my door. The first voice belonged to Aisling. "Really, Coco, if she wanted to come, she would have been in the lobby."

"But she said she might want to go. Maybe she fell asleep."

"Then we should let her sleep. She got in late last night."

Aisling was cut off by Coco knocking. "Piper? It's Coco. Don't you want to go downtown?"

I closed my journal and hauled myself off the bed. I opened the door to find Coco dressed in yet another outfit, this one a sleeveless pink shift dress and bright red heels. Aisling was standing behind her in a black minidress. She mouthed "sorry" to me and held up her hands.

"Don't you want to come with us?" Coco asked.

"I don't think so. I'm totally crashing."

"I told you, Coco," Aisling said, exasperated.

Coco looked at me and pouted.

I opened my mouth to repeat again I wasn't going, but I chided myself for acting like a hermit. Carabajel was supposed to be an adventure.

"Actually, I would love to go," I said. "I just need two seconds to put on some shoes."

Coco looked up and down at my outfit, which happened to be the same one I had been wearing all day. "Just shoes?" she asked.

"Just shoes," I replied.

One small thing I had neglected to consider was these girls and Gareth all had money—a lot of money. Aisling had somehow arranged a shuttle bus to bring us downtown, but we all had to cough up twenty dollars to pay for it, which ate up a good portion of my budget for the week.

The shuttle dropped us off right inside the wall on a street lined with shops. Like the night before, the carnival or celebration was going in full force a few blocks away. I stood on the curb and watched with fascination as the locals headed toward it. Everyone else was debating about where to have dinner, but I wanted to explore the tiny city. Besides, I didn't have the cash for what I presumed was going to be a fancy meal.

"I'll be back in time to meet the shuttle," I told Coco. She looked upset, but nodded, so I hurried down the street before she decided her essay would be in jeopardy if she didn't tail me throughout downtown.

As I walked through the crowded streets, I became distinctly aware that as soon as I got close to people, they would either dramatically stop and stare at me or leap out of my way.

When I came upon two guys about my age standing on a street corner, huddled together and whispering, one of them spotted me and pushed his friend who turned and looked at me in surprise. I smiled politely, trying to indicate I hadn't meant to intrude, but the first guy pulled his friend across the street in silence. I watched them resume their conversation again from a safe distance. The incident was disarming enough for me to pick up my pace, desperate to find one of the street vendors, grab a snack, and go back to find my group.

On the next corner, I found myself staring into a window of the most heavenly pastry shop I had ever seen. Cakes decorated with colorful sugar flowers lined the shelves along with tiny petit fours and cupcakes. The smell of sweet fresh bread alone did me in. It wouldn't be the healthiest dinner, but at least it would be cheap.

There was one customer at the counter in front of me, picking up what appeared to be a large order, given the number of boxes stacked before him. The shop-keeper was making quite a fuss over the man, and even with my limited Spanish, I could hear him thanking the man profusely for his business. The word "lider" was frequently tossed about, and the clerk certainly was groveling.

The man with the large order turned to leave, and the clerk glanced at me. He looked as startled by the sight of me as the people outside. I cleared my throat nervously and leaned down so I could see into the glass cases. A tray of chocolate and vanilla cupcakes deco-rated with black and purple icing looked too tempting to pass up.

"Uno," I struggled for the word for cupcake. "Cup-cake," I finally said in English and pointed to the display.

"Magdalena," the clerk said. "A cupcake es una magdalena en espanol."

He picked the largest black one from the tray and placed it on a small plate for me with a tiny fork. "Eat here? Comer aqui?"

I nodded. "Si. Gracias."

I paid him and took the plate over to a table by the window between a couple fussing over their baby and two older ladies in a heated disagreement about something. I had just peeled the wrapper off the cupcake and stuck my fork into it when the man with the large order burst back in through the door.

He was angry about something and began yelling at the clerk. The other customers in the store got very quiet, rose from their seats, and slipped out the door. In the case of the two women, their pastries were left uneaten on their plates. I glanced down at my cupcake and wondered if I should make my way to the exit too. I couldn't really blame the others. The man was a very imposing figure with his muscular arms and shaved head. From what I could understand, a box was missing from the order because he kept throwing out the numbers seven and eight.

The clerk was practically bowing as he rushed about, filling another box. He shook his arms, indicating something was in the back. The man waved him on impatiently and the clerk disappeared through a swinging door.

The man paced back and forth in front of the counter and then turned and looked around the room. He took in the empty chairs and the uneaten pastries without a care. But when his eyes came to rest on me, my hand poised in midair with a mouthful of cupcake on my fork, he jumped and took a step backward. Without a word, he grabbed the box and raced out of the store.

I looked down at the piece of cupcake still suspended halfway to my mouth. I put the fork back on the plate as a chill came over me. None of it made sense. First, a nun stared at me as though she knew me, then a man in a bakery ran at the very sight of me. Perhaps all of the Institute students were having the same problem. After all, the island had been isolated for decades, if not centuries.

Still, I couldn't help but wonder if something about me was completely offensive. I even considered that maybe my dreadlocks were sending the wrong message. But the customs officials at the airport hadn't been alarmed by my presence.

Then something occurred to me. *Hadn't I pulled up my lace hoodie before I got off the plane?*

I wasn't positive, but I was quite certain I had done so because I was afraid my hair was a mess. If so, then the problem was solved.

I couldn't help but giggle a little. I was used to people in authority reacting badly to my dreadlocks, but I'd certainly never intimidated a man who was three times my size.

The clerk reemerged from behind the swinging door carrying another box. He looked around the room, perplexed.

"He left," I said, pointing toward the window.

The clerk put the box down and wiped his brow with his apron.

I was slightly rattled by the episode, so I finished my cupcake as quickly as possible. When I stepped outside again, the street was desolate, and there was no sign of the man. I could hear the bells and chanting in the distance, but the street party must have moved farther away.

I started to retrace my steps back to where the shuttle dropped us off, looking for a store to buy something like a hat or kerchief to cover my hair.

I had just turned the corner when someone stepped out of the shadows and stood in front of me. He was by far the most attractive guy I had ever seen. He had wavy black hair and even darker eyes, and he was dressed entirely in black.

He looked at me intently with an arrogant smile on his face. I thought he was going to say hello, but instead he reached into his front shirt pocket and pulled out a pack of cigarettes. He lit one with a silver lighter and inhaled deeply, never once taking his eyes off mine.

A moment later, a tricked out black Humvee with shaded windows pulled up alongside him. Someone I couldn't see opened the passenger door from inside the car. The guy in black turned his back to me and swung himself inside, slamming the door shut behind him.

The Humvee took off, leaving me standing on the deserted street, baffled as to what, if anything, had just occurred.

❧ 6 ❧

The Invitation

The invitation arrived exactly one week later.

I was in the bathroom pulling my dreads into a ponytail when I heard a fumbling noise outside. I stepped into the little foyer and noticed someone had attempted to slip an envelope under my door, but it was so thick it had gotten stuck. I tried to pull it in to no avail, so I was forced to open my door and yank it out from the other side.

I looked up and down the hallway, expecting to see a messenger, but whoever had placed it there had disappeared.

I ran my fingers across the top of the envelope, surprised by its fancy elegance. It was cream-colored and made from a heavy cardstock. It reminded me of my dad's annual invitation to the Officers' Holiday Gala.

My name was written on the front in scrolling calligraphy. I assumed it was from the Institute, though no one had mentioned anything about a party. I closed the door and sat down on my bed to open it. Inside was a flimsy sheet of tissue paper protecting a small one-sided card. Engraved at the top in the center was a crest with two lions, and beneath it read *General Miguel Castillo*.

Dear Señorita Pfeiffer, it started in the same calligraphy as the envelope, and then the rest was in Spanish. I could make out most of the words—something about being cordially invited to the palace on Saturday at four o'clock.

I felt my stomach clench into a knot. *Tea with the leader of Carabajel? Weren't they taking the whole unofficial ambassador thing a bit far? And what could I possibly say to General Castillo? "Hi there, I'm Piper. Love your island, even if everyone is looking at me like I'm a freak of nature."*

With any luck, I could just hide behind my classmates and avoid having to speak to anyone. Surely, Aisling had gone to a million parties with presidents and could be counted on to make small talk.

My hand strayed up to my hair and I cringed. If dreadlocks were indeed a problem on Carabajel, there was no way I could go to the party without causing an international incident. I never had a chance to buy a scarf or a hat, and I was quite certain my collection of slightly tattered clothes in black or torn denim wasn't appropriate attire for the event.

That settles it, I thought. I'll tell Cecilia I have to be excused from attending.

When I finished getting dressed, I went downstairs to find her. She was standing by the breakfast buffet, pouring herself a coffee.

"Cecilia, it's a really nice invitation, but may I please be excused from this one event?"

Cecilia looked puzzled, so I handed her the envelope.

"My goodness!" she squealed as soon as she opened it. "The general invited you to tea!"

"You mean he didn't invite all of us?"

"All of you?"

"Everyone here with the Institute?"

"No. If he had, I'm sure someone would have told me by now."

"Wait a minute," I said, positive I hadn't heard her correctly. "You mean he only invited me? The president of Carabajel invited me to tea *alone*?"

Cecilia ran her hands over the raised gold crest admiringly. "We sent him a letter noting you were our essay winner. It was our hope he would acknowledge you in some way, but we had no idea he would invite you to his palace. Oh, Piper, what an honor."

Aisling and Gareth came over to us, holding their breakfast plates. "What honor?" Gareth asked.

"Piper has been invited to tea with General Castillo," Cecilia replied. "I am beside myself. It is such a great opportunity for us. And for Piper too. I will have to contact Enrique immediately."

"Who's Enrique?" I asked.

"The Institute's local assistant," she said.

Coco bounded over and put her arm around me. "Who's Enrique Castillo?"

I was about to explain, but Gareth beat me to it. "Not Enrique Castillo. General Castillo. Enrique is our liaison."

"Who's General Castillo?" Coco asked.

"He's the president of Carabajel and a ruthless dictator," Gareth replied.

Aisling rolled her eyes. "Someone over-studied."

"I felt it was my duty to learn about the island before we arrived, though there wasn't much on the Internet. This place is a cryptogram if you ask me."

"Who uses a word like 'cryptogram'?" Aisling asked.

"Gareth, apparently," I said. "We are getting way off topic."

Cecilia wasn't paying any attention to our bickering. "This is truly an honor," she repeated.

Aisling put her hands on her hips. "Poor little Piper, maybe he will show you his torture chamber."

"You're just jealous, Aisling," Coco said.

"Jealous of having lunch with a ruthless dictator? No, thank you, I will let Piper take this honor."

I covered my face with my hands, annoyed by the insanity. Cecilia was glowing, Aisling was green with jealousy, Coco was about to get into a fight with her, and the only thing no one had taken into account was there was no way I was going.

"I'm not going," I said.

Everyone responded at once, "Not going?"

"You have to go," Cecilia said. "This is what being a cultural language ambassador is all about."

"Then let someone else be a cultural ambassador at this event."

Gareth raised his hand. "I would be happy to take her place."

"He invited Piper," Coco protested.

"But Piper doesn't want to go," Aisling said.

Cecilia looked at me and then at the rest of the group. "Let's go somewhere we can talk, Piper."

She took my arm and led me outside to some chairs under one of the large blue umbrellas. Behind us, everyone dispersed, the excitement of the invitation quickly replaced with something else.

"Now, sweetie, tell me why you don't want to go," Cecilia said.

I hesitated, and then it all came out in a long rush. "Because it's not really my thing. I hate stuffy parties, I'm not good with protocol, and I have nothing to wear. And I think my hair is offending people down here."

"Gosh," Cecilia replied.

"There are a million good reasons to skip it and zero good reasons to go."

"I have a good reason—because he invited you. This is a huge opportunity. The man is highly reclusive and hates outsiders. He practically moves under the cover of darkness."

"How comforting."

"What I'm trying to say is things are changing around here. Last year, he opened the island to tourists, and this summer he let the Institute come here."

"Yes, but why me?"

"The scholarship, of course. And look at it this way. If he abruptly changes his mind about tourism, you will be one of the few people who can claim to have met him."

"What a privilege."

"He wants to meet with you, Piper. You simply have to go."

"Can't we send someone else? I'm really no good at these things, Cecilia. I'll make the Institute look bad."

"He invited you, not someone else."

"What if we send Aisling or Kimberlee and she calls herself Piper? The general will never know the difference, and I think Aisling or even Kimberlee could do a much better job representing us on a cultural mission."

"Piper, who knows how he would react if we ever got caught."

"I can't do it. Even if I did think I could go in there

and hold a conversation, what about my clothes and my hair?"

Cecilia pulled on one of my dreadlocks thoughtfully. "You know, what about asking the other girls to borrow something?"

"No way. I don't dress like a macaroon."

Cecilia giggled. "I admit they are a little," she paused, "overdone for the tropics."

"A little?"

"What about something from my closet? I have a few simple black dresses. If we pin the back, we can probably make one of them fit. Leave your attire to me."

She handed me back the invitation. I sat there pouting in silence, feeling defeated. Cecilia watched me with a patient smile.

"Fine," I finally said. "I'll go. But do I have to notify someone? Tell them I will attend, I mean?" From what I could tell, there was nothing indicating how to R.S.V.P.

Cecilia took the invitation out of my hands and translated it into English.

Dear Miss Pfeiffer, You are cordially invited to join General Miguel Castillo at the Palacio de Santa Barbara this Saturday, June 30th, at four o'clock in the afternoon. For your convenience, a driver will escort you a quarter hour before. Regards, Graciela Esteban, Secretary to General Miguel Castillo.

"See?" Cecilia said. "There is no opportunity to

decline. When General Castillo invites someone over, they go."

She handed the invitation back to me and I shoved it into my purse. "I have no idea what I am going to say to this guy," I told her.

"You can start by telling him wonderful things about this Institute. This could be a great fundraising opportunity for us, you know."

***

SATURDAY CAME ALL TOO QUICKLY, AND MAKING matters worse, we were experiencing a monsoon. But I was too distracted by my closet to worry about the weather. I moved a few hangers back and forth, as if a ball gown would magically appear. I assumed Cecilia forgot she had promised to lend me a dress, and I was too embarrassed to remind her.

I'd brought two black knit dresses to Carabajel, but the one I wore the day I arrived was balled up in my laundry pile and still smelled like an airplane. The other one had a white skull embroidered across the front. Even my jeans were completely unacceptable. The ones without holes in the knees had holes in the upper thigh, and the ones without those holes were missing a pocket in the back. It wasn't my fault I had a Shiba Inu who thought jeans were tasty.

It would have to be the skull dress then. I pulled on

a pair of black tights and was wiggling into the dress when I heard a knock on my door. Cecilia stood on the other side holding a large canvas bag. She looked me up and down and frowned.

"A skull is not quite the statement we want to make right now," she said.

"I thought you forgot."

"Of course not. Piper, this man is very important, and you will be representing the Institute. I'm sure I have something with me that you will feel comfortable wearing."

She reached into her bag and pulled out a few dresses. I was surprised they actually didn't make me cringe. All of them were simply cut and none of the fabric itched when I touched it. Out of the three items she brought with her, I chose a dark blue one with a high neckline and bell sleeves. It was about two sizes too big for me, but she had also remembered to bring safety pins.

"Turn around," she ordered when I stepped out of the bathroom wearing her dress. She did something with the pins in the back so the dress didn't hang off me like a potato sack.

"See, isn't this better?" she asked.

I looked in the full-length mirror on the back of the bathroom door and had to admit she was right.

"Thanks so much, Cecilia, I'm really grateful. But what about my hair?"

She grinned and reached back into her bag. "Not to worry. I am going to make a nice bun."

She pulled my hair into a high ponytail and tried to hide the streak of pale pink the stylist in Jersey had given me before I left. I watched her in the mirror and was quite impressed with her work. I would have to remember the style when I got back home because my dad was always embarrassed by my hair whenever we attended an event on base.

When Cecilia was finished fastening my dreads with bobby pins, she gathered up a small piece of gray lace with little pink roses embroidered on it. When she looped it over the top of my head and tied it at the nape of my neck, it looked as though I had the same hair as everyone else.

"It's perfect," I said. "Thank you, Cecilia. Really."

She patted my head in mock authority. "I completely understand. Now remember to say nice things about the Institute if he asks."

"Sure, yes, of course I will."

At twenty-five to four, I locked my door behind us, and we went downstairs to stand under the lobby carport. There was no sign of the other girls and Gareth, and I was glad. The last thing I wanted was to make a spectacle of myself.

Cecilia looked up at the sky. "I can't believe this weather," she said. "The weather bureau said it is going to be a bad hurricane season. This must be the start of it."

"My dad mentioned the hurricanes. He's a weather fanatic. You have to be when you fly all the time."

"Sounds glamorous."

"It's not. He flies medical supplies around for the Air Force."

"Look, here comes his car now," she said, pointing to the road.

Any lingering hope I had about the entire tea party thing being a joke was dashed when a black sedan with tinted windows turned into the long drive and headed toward us.

"How do you know it's his car?" I asked, even though the question was stupid. No one else but a general would be rolling around the island in a car the size of a small tank when everyone else drove junkers.

Before Cecilia could respond, the driver's side door opened and a stout man wearing a chauffeur's uniform stepped out and approached us. He looked right at me and said, "Señorita Pfeiffer?"

"Yes," I replied.

"I am Carlos, General Castillo's driver."

"This is Cecilia Delano, our instructor," I said. They exchanged a few pleasantries in Spanish, most of which I was thrilled to realize I actually understood.

"Are you ready, señorita?" he asked.

I wasn't, but I nodded anyway.

"I'll stop by your room later," Cecilia told me.

"Okay, and thanks again." I touched the cuff of her dress and she winked.

Carlos held the back door open for me and I slid in onto a cold, maroon leather seat. The air conditioning was blasting despite the chilly, wet weather, so I rubbed my arms together for warmth.

After he closed the door, I tried to wave to Cecilia, but the windows were shaded from the inside too. With the exception of the front windshield, I could barely see a thing.

I tried to keep my bearings as we drove away from the campus, but Carlos made so many turns, it was impossible for me to follow the route. I could tell we were climbing, though. The road was gradually sloping upward at a steep angle. Every so often we approached a sharp curve and Carlos nearly had to stop the car in order to make the turn. After a few more of his maneuvers, I didn't have any lingering doubt. We were definitely heading up a mountain.

The landscape changed from palm trees and low scrub bushes to thick, immense foliage. The driving rain was tapering off, and a heavy fog was descending around the car.

After what felt like an eternity, we passed the ruins of an old lookout tower and Carlos turned left onto a paved driveway. Midway down the road, we came to a gatehouse where four men in uniform were keeping watch. I was used to armed guards from the Air Force, but I was still slightly alarmed by the huge machine guns strapped diagonally across their shoulders.

Carlos drove past them without slowing down, but he flashed the high beams of the car three times in very rapid succession.

"Almost there, señorita," he said. "The palace is up ahead."

I bit the edge of my thumb's cuticle like I always do when I'm nervous. Through the mist I caught a glimpse of lights, and then a towering fountain came into view, water shooting out of the mouths of six intertwined sailfish.

Carlos stopped the car on the other side of the fountain and turned off the ignition. "Here we are," he said.

I strained to see the house, but the angle at which he had parked the car hid it from my view. I reached for my door handle, but it was locked.

"I'll get your door, señorita," he told me.

He came around to my side, holding an umbrella over my head. In front of me was a chateau with a slate roof and four pointed towers, their spires barely visible in the fog. The chateau looked out of place in the midst of the jungle, as though it had been picked up by a tornado in France and deposited in the middle of a rain forest.

Carlos took my elbow and led me up the stone steps.

He opened the massive front door without knocking, and we entered a vast foyer with a black-and-white tiled floor and ornate gold furniture. There was no one else in sight, and the place was as silent as a tomb.

Still holding my arm, Carlos shuttled me across the foyer and through a peach-colored room with a large piano and a harp by the window. He opened a door on the far side of the room, and I followed him into a dining room. In the center was a rectangular table with about twenty chairs around it. Silk tapestries painted with cherry blossoms lined the walls, and two men were standing beside the table, speaking to someone I couldn't see. They must have heard us enter the room because they abruptly stopped talking and stepped backward.

At the head of the table sat an extraordinarily handsome man. He was deeply tanned with thick silver hair brushed back from his forehead. He was wearing the same black military uniform as the customs officials at the airport, except his was heavily decorated with multi-colored pins and thicker gold lapels.

"General, may I present Señorita Ruth Pfeiffer from the United States of America," Carlos said, but General Castillo was already pushing his chair back and standing up.

For a second, there was an awkward silence in the room. Then he uttered only two words.

"My God."

7

The General's Palace

We stood there, staring at each other. I was dumbfounded as to what to do next, but the general quickly regained his composure and extended his hand.

"Miss Pfeiffer, it is a pleasure to make your acquaintance," he said. When he released my hand, he bowed slightly. I wasn't sure if I was supposed to curtsy or bow in return, but it felt unnatural, so I nodded and waited for him to say something more. But instead of speaking, he just scrutinized me with an expression of either surprise or disbelief.

After an interminable moment, he finally motioned for me to sit down at the table. He pulled the gilded chair to his right out for me, and I sat down as gracefully as I could manage. When I leaned back, one of Cecilia's pins must have come undone because I felt something stab me in the back. I sat up quickly and folded my hands in my lap, pretending I had been trying to master perfect posture.

The general sat down too, but he was still gazing at me as though trying to memorize my face. I looked over my shoulder and noticed the other men had disappeared along with Carlos. The only sound was the crackle of wood burning in a fireplace behind his chair.

"Thank you for coming," he said.

"Thank you for the invitation, General Castillo." I attempted to match his formal tone.

We sat in silence for a few minutes longer and I tried not to fidget. I wondered if I was the one who was supposed to make conversation with him, but my instincts warned me the guest of a ruler should only speak when spoken to.

"Would you care for some coffee or tea?" he asked.

"Coffee would be great. Thank you."

He reached across the table and rang a small silver bell. I didn't think people actually still used those things. We waited, but no one arrived. He rang the bell again. Still nothing. I noticed his hands were rough and calloused as though he had been out cutting a crop. He rang the bell furiously a third time.

"This thing never works," he said.

I looked down at the table and tried not to giggle.

"I am sorry, Miss Pfeiffer. My staff works very hard, but this is a large house."

"It is very beautiful," I said.

"We refer to the Santa Barbara as a palace, but it is actually a chateau. It was built for a beautiful woman."

"Was she from France?" I asked, wondering if he was talking about his wife.

"No, but she loved France, so I ordered plans from an architect in Paris, and our island craftsmen duplicated it to the very last detail."

I waited for him to say something more about his chateau, but we slipped back into an awkward silence. When I couldn't take it anymore, I said absurdly, "My father is in the Air Force."

"The Air Force?"

"Yes, in the medical supply corps."

"I find medicine so interesting. Although I have never had the chance to study anything more than military tactics. I am sure you know my history."

I didn't see any point in lying. "I'm sorry, no. I'd never heard of Carabajel before the International Language Institute. I did try to do a little research before I arrived, but there was not much I could find besides the black sugar."

The general smiled. "See, you know more about the island than most people on this earth. Our black sugar is quite valuable. Every month, the Carabajelians receive a check from the earnings of the exportation. I believe everyone who lives here is entitled to share in the wealth."

"That's so nice of you."

Something crashed to the floor, and the general and I both jumped in our seats. A woman wearing a purple dress with a ruffled white apron was standing in the doorway holding a silver tray at a slant that had caused a cup and saucer to hit the floor. Instead of taking stock of the mess, she was gawking at me.

"Clara," the general said. His voice was low and firm. She looked at him first and then back at me, her mouth agape.

Okay, this time it can't be my hair, I thought.

The general stood up, and I followed his lead.

"Don't worry, Miss Pfeiffer, you can sit down," the general said, but I ignored him and kept standing.

Clara bent down on the floor, apologizing profusely in Spanish, the tray balancing on her knees. I thought he was going to start yelling at the poor woman, but instead he stood there stoically and watched her try to clean up the mess.

"I really don't need any coffee," I said. "I am really okay."

Clara peeked at me and nodded. Then to my utter surprise, she regained her footing and bowed to me.

"Go back to the kitchen, Clara, thank you," the

general said. He took the tray from her hands and placed it on the table.

"Please sit," he said to me, and this time I did.

There were two silver pots on the tray along with a sugar bowl and a creamer. He poured coffee from one of the pots into the remaining cup and saucer and placed it in front of me.

"Cream?"

"Yes, please."

"Sugar?"

"Sure, thank you."

"It is, of course, our black sugar." He opened the top of the sugar bowl and, using the tiny spoon wedged into a cleft on the side, scooped out a teaspoon of black sugar that sparkled like tiny diamonds.

I stirred my coffee and then sipped it. The sugar added a distinctive flavor. I expected it to be like licorice, but instead it reminded me of lavender.

The general was obviously waiting for a reaction, so I put the cup back down on the saucer and looked at him.

"Delicious," I said.

"Thank you," he replied, obviously pleased.

"Thank you for acknowledging the contest. The Intercultural Language Institute is really glad to be here," I said, remembering my promise to Cecilia.

"What contest?" he asked.

"The essay contest," I began slowly. *Wasn't my scholar-*

ship the reason I was invited to the palace? "I won the schol-arship to attend the Institute."

"Oh, right. Yes, yes, of course. Your parents must be proud."

"My father is, in his own way. My mother died when I was four."

"I'm so sorry. A tragedy indeed."

"It's okay. I wish I could say I remember her. But I don't. Just some fragmented images here and there."

"Still," he replied and then his face visibly darkened. "Loss, it is our deepest suffering."

"Yes."

Another uncomfortable lapse ensued before he leaned closer and lowered his voice. "So, you had never heard of Carabajel before this contest of sorts?"

"No, I'm sorry," I told him. "I needed to learn Spanish because I'm going to Vassar, Vassar College, in the fall. I entered the essay contest and won, and here I am."

"Are you certain?"

I wasn't sure what he was getting at. *Was I certain I had never heard of the island? Or was I certain I won the contest?*

Either way, the answer was the same. "Yes, I am absolutely certain," I replied.

"It is a coincidence then, I am sure."

"I'm sorry, what's a coincidence?"

He pushed his chair back, stood up, and walked over

to the window. Outside, the rain had started again, and the sky looked prematurely dark with all the fog.

Still facing the window, he spoke emphatically. "I am an educated man, Miss Pfeiffer, and until this point, fate and fortune had very little to do with my life. The Carabajelians are a wonderful, proud people, and they have been isolated for a long time in a crystal dome."

"A crystal dome?"

"Only an expression, my dear. Their superstitions were never ones I shared. Until now, that is."

I was completely befuddled. "I am sorry, General Castillo, I'm not sure I'm following you."

When he turned back to me, I was surprised to see beneath his distinguished bearing, there was a look of sadness on his face. "Yes, I can see you do not. Perhaps it is for the best. And if you will indulge me for a moment, I would like to say I am grateful for your ignorance."

The general walked over to the table and rang the silver bell. "Miss Pfeiffer, our interview is over. Carlos will be here momentarily to bring you back to your residence." He nodded at me once, and then turned and stormed out of the room.

After he disappeared, I shivered. Despite the fire burning in the fireplace, the draft in the room had gotten worse. I stared at the flames and wondered why they weren't giving off enough heat. I was about to push my chair back when I looked up to see Clara standing in the doorway where the general had exited.

She looked over both her shoulders before rushing toward me and reaching for my hand. She whispered something that sounded like "santarella," and she pressed a small piece of wood with beads attached to it into my palm. Before I could respond, she recoiled and dashed back through the door.

I opened my hand and looked down. She had given me a rosary made from lacquered black beads. Even the crucifix was black. I'd left my purse in my room because it was so worn, so I didn't know what to do with the rosary other than put it around my neck and tuck it into my dress.

I walked over to the doorway she had used and felt my eyes widen with surprise. The room before me was breathtaking. It was a glass-enclosed courtyard with a fountain in the center and marble columns reaching all the way to the second floor. Palm trees, their trunks wrapped with little white lights, stood between the columns. Everywhere I looked, black flowers were draped over railings and planted in flower boxes on the floor.

"Clara?" I whispered. But there was no sign of her.

I stepped back into the dining room, and when I turned slightly to my left, I saw Carlos standing in the far doorway. I wasn't sure how long he had been there or if he had witnessed the scene with Clara.

"Follow me, Señorita Pfeiffer," he said.

I trailed him back through the peach room with the harp and piano, and then into the foyer of the front door. He opened the door and let me pass through it before him.

The general's black sedan was idling on the circular drive at the foot of the steps. I thought Carlos was going to drive me back to the dorm, but he only opened the passenger door for me, waited for me to slide inside, and then closed it behind me with a slam. Another driver wearing a chauffeur's hat was sitting behind the wheel. Carlos tapped on the roof of the car, and the driver put the car in gear.

The new driver was totally focused on the road in front of him, but it wasn't until we passed the guardhouse that I found the courage to slip the rosary back over my head. I inspected it closely to see if there was any marking on it or any clue at all as to why Clara had given it to me. But as far as I could tell, it looked like an ordinary rosary.

"I hope you don't mind," the driver said, "but I'm going to have to drive a bit slower than usual because the rain and fog make the roads up here treacherous."

"No, I don't mind," I lied because I minded quite a bit. I wanted to get as far away from the general and his peculiar palace as quickly as humanly possible.

I leaned my head back against the cold leather seat. The entire episode from start to finish was unsettling. I wasn't sure if it had gone well or if I was going to wake up in a Carabajel prison.

I also had no idea how I was going to describe what transpired to Cecilia. Nothing added up. We had assumed he'd invited me to the palace because I won the essay contest, but instead he acted as if he knew nothing about it. *And why did he say, "My God" when he first saw me? And why did Clara give me a rosary of all things?*

When we finally and blessedly reached the campus entrance, I still had no answers. I was about to direct the driver to my dorm, but he knew exactly which building mine was. He stopped the car and got out to open the back door for me.

"It was nice to meet you, Miss Pfeiffer," he said, bowing so low his chauffeur's hat covered much of his face.

"Gracias," I mumbled.

The black car drove off, and I watched it go with a confused sigh. I looked up at the sky. The dark clouds had finally parted, and the rain had stopped.

I hurried up the exterior staircase of the dorm. When I reached my door, I whirled around irrationally, half expecting to see someone watching me. But the hallway was deserted. Still, I slammed the door closed behind me and bolted the top lock. I was about to unzip Cecilia's dress when a gripping realization came over me.

The driver.

I had seen him before. He was the furious man in the café who picked up the huge pastry order. I had surprised him or shocked him that night. *Did that mean he had something to do with my invitation to the palace?*

8

Terror in the Library

Later that evening, Cecilia knocked on my door, but I didn't answer. She even called my name a few times, but I didn't want to talk to her or anyone else. I was lying on my bed with the lights off, replaying the events of the day. I was also starving, but I didn't dare go downstairs and face questions from Gareth and the other girls.

Everything about Carabajel was bothering me. I would have given anything to get a call out to my dad, but the pay phone in the lobby was still in serious need of repair. All I heard when I picked up the receiver was a low hissing noise. And pressing zero did absolutely nothing.

When Cecilia finally stopped knocking, I got up,

turned the light on, and sat down at my desk. I rummaged through my backpack until I found the journal Becky had given me, and then I started to write down my thoughts. I couldn't ignore it any longer. Something was definitely going on with the island. First, there was the déjà vu when I arrived, then the puzzled looks from the locals, including the nun on the beach, then the bizarre meeting with the general and, finally, the rosary scene with Clara.

Even after writing everything down, nothing made any more sense. I rested my chin in my palms. Someone had to have the answers I was looking for, but I was operating in the dark without the Internet. Then it hit me. I was an idiot for not coming up with it sooner. *A library.* I would just have to research the island the old way.

Rejuvenated, I walked over to the closet and pulled Cecilia's dress off the hangar. I freshened up quickly and headed out across campus to the first octagon building where Cecilia was staying.

She swung open her door before I even finished knocking. "Piper! I was getting worried about you."

"Sorry, I fell asleep when I got back. I wanted to return your dress." I handed it to her, and she draped it over her forearm.

"Well, come in, come in. I want to hear all about your afternoon."

She ushered me inside, and I sat down on an overstuffed sofa in front of her television. Her apartment was huge in comparison to my room. From what I could tell, it had three bedrooms and a massive balcony outside that ran the entire length of the living room. She sat down on the chair across from me and raised her eyebrows as though I was about to say the most interesting thing in the world. "So, what happened? Tell me everything."

"Oh, not much." I tried to sound casual. "He was very polite, we had coffee, and he congratulated me on my essay."

She clasped her hands together. "How wonderful! I will tell Enrique first thing on Monday. We need to send the general a thank you note. I still say there is a fundraising opportunity in all of this."

I nodded even though I wasn't so sure. "Um, Cecilia, I was wondering, is there a library around here somewhere? I thought maybe I'd look for an additional place to study or get a book."

I could tell Cecilia was still thinking about my meeting with the general because she was starting to scribble notes down on a yellow pad.

"A library? I think it used to be on the other side of campus behind the large blue-and-white administration building. I'm not sure if it is open, though. And there must be one in Carabajel City somewhere."

I stood up, and she didn't try to stop me. "Thanks again for the dress."

"Anytime, Piper," she said. She stopped writing and looked up at me. "You know, I'm really glad you're here. I've noticed you tend to keep to yourself, but I'm sure in the next few weeks you'll feel closer to the other girls."

I smiled. Becoming closer to the other girls, I thought as I closed her apartment door behind me, was about the very last thing on my mind.

When I left Cecilia's apartment, darkness had descended, and without the moon, the campus was pitch black. I decided to wait until morning before I attempted to find the library. Besides going to class, the saltwater pool, and my one trip down to the beach, I hadn't explored the rest of the school grounds. I didn't even know where to locate the blue-and-white administration building Cecilia had mentioned.

Back in my room, I opened the balcony door for air, put on my favorite nightshirt, and climbed into bed. I stayed awake, staring at the ceiling, hearing the general's voice, over and over, expressing his gratitude for my ignorance. *But ignorance of what?* It was maddening.

At some point during the night, I had a dream. I was on a pier in a cove surrounded by mountains. A torch burned at the end of the pier, and a dark-haired man wearing the same uniform as the general stood beneath it. I couldn't see his face because his back was to me, but I started to run toward him. Then I woke up.

The dream was nothing, but for some reason I

couldn't fall asleep again, so I lay in bed shivering until the sun came up. I was overcome by the desire to talk to someone normal, someone who wasn't linked to the island. But even if I had been able to reach my father, I knew he would just tell me my imagination was out of control.

I dressed in my usual uniform of black shorts and a tank top and stuffed my journal and pen into my backpack. Outside, it was warmer than it had been in days and the sun was shining brightly, even though it was only eight o'clock. Pilar was setting up the breakfast buffet when I walked into the lobby, so I picked up a guava pastry and a few napkins to take with me.

I went out the back door and followed the paved path through the gardens toward the cluster of stucco buildings where the college classes took place. Midway there, I found a campus map mounted on a large sign protected by clear plastic. The library was exactly where Cecilia had said it would be—right behind the administration building.

The campus was deserted, and the stillness was making me a little anxious. The only sound came from the rustling of the palm fronds in the wind and the waves hitting the seawall. The entire place had a look of desolation. I guessed the library would probably be locked, but when I tried the door, it opened easily. The lights were off, but sun blazed in through the floor-to-ceiling windows on one side.

I had to stop for a minute to consider what my next move was going to be. I looked around to see if there was a security guard or clerk on duty somewhere who was going to give me a hard time for trespassing. The Institute hadn't given us any student identification cards, so the only thing I had in my wallet was my New Jersey driver's license, which I assumed wasn't going to do me much good. But the place seemed to be empty.

I walked past the circulation desk and into the main room where bookshelves were lined up in an incredibly disorganized fashion. Practically none of them were the same size, and they appeared as though they had been added at different times, without any sense of grouping order. The base library on Sandy Point may have been too regimented, but at least it had structure.

I walked amongst the shelves, trying to see if I could find a pattern, but it was nearly impossible without translating every Spanish title. Finally, I spotted several long wooden cabinets with tiny drawers and brass handles along the far wall. But when I pulled the drawers open, they were stuffed with index cards that had no discernible order.

The other cabinets proved more useful. One had a sign above it that read, *General Catalog—Subject*, and the other read *General Catalog—Author*. Since I didn't have the first clue about any local authors, I opened the subject drawer and went straight to the history section. I flipped through the sections marked *Caribbean History,*

European History, and *Latin American History* until I came to a divider with *Carabajel History* typed on the tab.

There weren't many books listed, but I pulled out my journal and wrote down the title that sounded like it could help me the most because it was one of the only ones listed as being in English. *The Saints of Carabajel.*

The card said it had been written over ten years ago, but at least it was a start. I jotted down the call number, and after looking for what felt like an eternity, I finally found the English-language books on the second floor, on the opposite side of the wall with the windows.

The Saints of Carabajel was on the third shelf from the bottom at the end of the row. It was a thin book, and it was filled with photographs of women holding crosses or pictured in some stance of prayer. When I flipped through the pages, I also saw a photograph of General Castillo in his younger days wearing his uniform and standing next to an older man wearing the same uniform. The caption under the photograph read, "Maximo and Miguel Castillo." I assumed from the similarities in their features that Maximo Castillo was the general's father or uncle.

I held the book in my hands and considered what I should do with it since no one was working the circulation desk. A few feet away from the shelves where I was standing, there was a small desk facing the wall. Rather than leaving with the book, I decided to read a few chapters first.

No sooner had I sat down and turned to the part about the general than I heard a whining creak. Don't be a loser, it's only the wind outside, I told myself. I'd spent lots of time restocking alone in Sandy Point's dark library after hours. It was always fairly spine-chilling.

I was just about to look down at the book again when I saw—or at least I was quite certain I saw—a shadow cross the wall to my right.

I froze and held my breath, listening.

There was another creak and the unmistakable sound of floorboards bending under someone's footsteps. Someone was coming toward me very slowly. My first instinct was to run. My second instinct was to hide.

I glanced around quickly. Hiding was definitely not an option. The shelves couldn't provide any cover, and the desk I was sitting at was too small to crawl underneath. I grabbed the book and my purse and stood up quietly.

The creaking continued, but the library was so cavernous, I couldn't tell if the sound was coming from the first or second floor.

The second floor wasn't much of a floor. It was really just a balcony that wrapped around the perimeter of the building. To my left, I saw the emergency exit stairs, and without giving it another thought, I tiptoed as fast as I could toward them.

The staircase was pitch black, except for the blinking emergency exit signs. I dashed down the stairs, pushed the metal door open softly, and then stopped.

Someone was standing between me and the front door. The profile of a man dressed in dark clothing vanished behind a shelf.

I looked around frantically for another door. I had come down an emergency exit staircase after all, but apparently it only led people to the front door because there was nothing around me except windows and walls.

I crouched down behind the closest shelf and pulled out a few books so I could see. It occurred to me that maybe I was being ridiculous. *What if he was just a security guard?*

I thought quickly about all of my self-defense training, all those military classes my dad made me take. "You never know," he always said. Now I was in a situation where I might have to use the training, and I couldn't remember a thing.

I turned my head, hoping to hear something, but the library was silent.

Come on, Piper, be reasonable. Why would a random person be after you?

I waited a few more seconds and then stood up and crept toward a high shelf. I carefully removed two more books. The next thing I heard was my own scream. Two dark eyes were staring at me from the other side.

9

Julian

The only thing louder than my own scream was the scream of the guy standing on the other side of the shelf. With a force I didn't know I possessed, I thrust the rest of the books between us into his face.

The entire bookcase started to topple over, and there was a loud crashing noise followed by, "Owww, Jesus!"

But I wasn't about to stick around. I raced out of the aisle and bounded toward the library door.

"Espera, espera," the guy yelled behind me, but I couldn't remember the translation. *Stop? Wait?* I wasn't about to do either.

I had just passed the circulation desk and was about

to open the glass door when I felt a hand on my shoulder.

"Get away from me," I cried. I spun around and slammed the book into his forehead.

He grabbed my wrist and wouldn't let go. "Señorita, miss, please por favor, stop attacking me. I'm not trying to hurt you."

My heart was pounding as I tried to free myself, but I had to admit he appeared more pained and puzzled than dangerous.

Then I recognized him. He was the handsome guy who had stepped out of the shadows on the sidewalk on my first night downtown. If he remembered me too, he gave no indication.

"Can I let go of your hand?" he asked. "Will you stop trying to brain me with your book?"

I nodded and he carefully released the pressure on my wrist. He smiled down at me. "I'm sorry I startled you," he said in perfect, somewhat British-tinged English. "I thought I was alone in the library."

"And when you found out you weren't, you thought it was a good idea to sneak up on the other person?" I asked.

My tone wiped the smile off his face. "Sneak up on you? You snuck up on me. What were you doing hiding behind a shelf?"

"I wasn't hiding. What were *you* doing in the library?"

He raised an eyebrow. "Hmm, I don't know, looking for a book? What else does one do in a library?"

I opened my mouth to respond, but I didn't have a comeback. "Well, you still shouldn't sneak up on someone," I snapped.

To my surprise, he laughed. "Fine, the next time I'm in a public institution in broad daylight where I have every right to be, I will be sure to announce my presence in case there is another super doll hiding out behind shelving."

"Did you just call me a super doll?"

"It's fitting. I didn't expect a girl as tiny as you to have the superhuman strength to take out a shelf of dictionaries and then nearly knock me out. I'm Julian, by the way."

"Piper."

"What a unique name."

"My name is really Ruth, but everyone calls me Piper."

He looked perplexed, so I added, "My last name is Pfeiffer."

"But Ruth is a beautiful name. Anyway, I'm pleased to meet you, Piper. You are here with the International Language Institute?"

"How do you know?" I asked, folding my arms across my chest.

"It's summer. Only the Institute students are here."

"You aren't an Institute student, so what are you doing here?"

"I'm sorry, I should have been more specific. Only the Institute students and I are here during the summer. I keep my dorm room year-round. I just finished my third year here. I'm in the pre-med program." He ran his fingers through his thick black hair and eyed me. "If you don't mind me saying so, you are a bit jumpy."

I felt my shoulders sag. "It's been a curious week."

"Don't feel bad, it's a curious island."

"You think so too?"

"Yes, I think it's curious even though it's my home." He hesitated for a moment. "Well, it's sort of my home. Not really, but I was born here and grew up here. I'm rambling, aren't I?"

"Yes."

"All right, long story short. I was born here, but I attended boarding school in England most of my life. My mother died when I was born so my father sent me off as soon as I was old enough."

"I'm sorry. We have something in common."

"What's that?"

"My mother died when I was four."

"I'm terribly sorry too."

"It's okay. I don't remember her."

"I was too young to remember my mother too, obviously. Anyway, now I'm back here to attend the university. After I graduate, I'm going to medical school in the States. Hopefully Harvard."

"Good for you." It came out cheekier than I'd meant, but he didn't seem to notice.

"What about you? Where are you from?"

"The States."

He waited for me to elaborate, or perhaps name a particular state, but I didn't feel like explaining my vagabond existence.

"And you were looking for a book?" he asked. "Presumably, this one?" He reached down and tilted my wrist to see the book's cover. His nose wrinkled in disgust. "What do you want with this trash?"

"I was looking for some island history."

"That book is nothing but superstitious idiocy. If it is history you are after, you should keep looking."

I shrugged, vaguely offended my choice of book had caused such a reaction. "I want this one," I said. "And since no one is at the circulation desk to help me check it out, I'm going to take it."

"Good. Get it out of here."

"I do plan on returning it when I'm done."

"No need. Throw it out." He held the glass door open for me. "You know, when I was a kid and used to come home for summers, the island was magical, coming from dreary England. But now, things once magical feel backward. And, well..."

"It's complicated?" I offered.

He grinned. "Yeah, it's complicated."

I smiled back at him. It was nice to talk to someone other than my classmates, who probably wouldn't even notice if the island burned down around them.

Then, out of nowhere, I felt a wave of self-consciousness wash over me. I most definitely looked like a sweaty mess, and I was beginning to feel mortified about the whole library incident. Suddenly, it was all too much. The fancy girls, the nun, the general and his horrid chauffeur, Clara and her rosary. And then the most uncharacteristic thing happened. My eyes filled with tears.

"Hey, are you okay?" he asked. He reached into his pocket and pulled out a white handkerchief. I felt bad taking it, so I just smiled and shook my head. I'd never met a guy who carried a handkerchief before.

"Thanks," I managed. "Sorry."

"There is nothing to be sorry for. I'm the one who should be apologizing. I didn't mean to scare you the way I did. If it makes you feel any better, you almost gave me a stroke. And a black eye."

"I'm really sorry I pushed the books onto you and hit you."

"It's all right. I shouldn't have chased you, but like I said, I didn't expect to see such a pretty girl on the other side of the dictionary shelf. Then you pushed the shelf over and I couldn't imagine what happened. Now, seriously, are you all right?"

"Yes, I'm okay now," I lied.

"Are you sure?"

I felt like I needed to sit down. "No," I admitted. "No, I am not okay."

He took my arm. "You'll probably feel better if you rest for a second. Even with my limited medical knowledge, I can tell you might be on the verge of hyperventilating."

I let him lead me over to the seawall, and we sat on the edge under the shade of a giant palm tree. The rocks felt cool under my legs, and thankfully the sun was hiding behind some clouds. I had stopped crying, but my breath kept getting caught in my chest.

"Why don't you talk to me?" he asked gently. "Tell me in a long sentence who you are."

"A long sentence?"

"Trust me."

"Okay. I am here to study Spanish because I am going to Vassar in the fall, and I need to be fluent in a second language or I won't be allowed to register, and I live in New Jersey right now, but it's not really my home because my dad is in the Air Force and we move around a lot, and I spent most of my childhood out west."

"Where out west?"

"Alaska, Wyoming, Nevada, Texas, and New Mexico."

"Where did you like it best?"

"I don't know. Texas, maybe. I liked Dallas."

"See, you are feeling better, are you not?"

I nodded. "Yeah, I think so. Thanks."

"Long sentences always help calm patients down." He was smiling kindly at me.

"You're going to be a good doctor."

"Thank you. I hope so. How do you like Carabajel so far?"

"Honestly?" I asked.

"Yes, honestly."

"It's beautiful. It's the most beautiful place I have ever seen. But a few strange things have happened since I arrived, and I think I finally broke down."

"Strange? What do you mean?"

I was about to reply, but instead I gripped his forearm without realizing it. Over his shoulder, several yards away, was a nun. She was standing at the far edge of the seawall, watching us.

Julian turned and followed my gaze. "What's wrong?" he asked.

"The nun. Do you see her?"

"I see her, all right. She is one of the Black Mariahs."

When she saw that we had noticed her, she turned and disappeared into the foliage.

"What's a Black Mariah?"

"That's the name of their order. They have a powerful following here. Unfortunately," he added.

"The other day I took a walk on the beach, and one

of them appeared out of nowhere. I didn't see her at first, but she saw me."

"Are you sure?"

I nodded.

"She didn't say anything or try to talk to you?"

"No. I thought she was going to, but then she took off in the other direction. I ran for my life."

"Very smart move on your part."

"Why?"

He rubbed his chin and seemed to be pondering his next words. "They are both dangerous and not dangerous," he said. "I don't think they would hurt you physically, but they might try and convince you of lies like the ones they tell to the Carabajelians."

"What's their problem?"

"The Black Mariahs believe Carabajel is their island, and they are constantly plotting and holding small rebellions. The other day they sabotaged an entire construction site out by the airport."

"But why would they want to talk to me if I'm not from here?"

"I'm sure they would welcome the opportunity to plead their case to outsiders if given the chance. Would you do me a favor, Piper?"

"Sure."

"If you see them, get away. Don't talk to them, and don't let them talk to you."

"This is getting serious."

"I'm trying to save you the trouble of having to listen to their nonsense. You will walk away, right?"

"Okay."

"Good. In fact, it's probably best if you avoid the entire area around their convent."

"Where is it?"

He gestured to the left where a small hill plunged into the sea. "Over there beyond the next cove. If you listen carefully on a quiet day, you can hear the sound of their bells."

"No wonder she was on the beach then, if their convent is close by. Oh, and this nun was shockingly beautiful too. Like a movie star."

"Malfaedra probably. She is the most stunning of the group, though a lot of them are quite beautiful. They recruit the prettiest girls of Carabajel and convert them to the order. The sick thing is the families actually believe it is a great honor for their daughters to be chosen."

"The families here want their daughters to be nuns?" It sounded like such a confining notion.

Julian nodded. "Some girls go in as young as age thirteen and don't leave the convent for years. When they do appear again, they are, how would you say, different?"

"Sounds awful. And no one can stop it?"

"No. There are some things about this island too ingrained to be changed. My father tries to stop the rebellions every chance he gets, but as soon as one is over, another one springs up."

"Wait, did you say your father tries to shut down the rebellions?"

"He tries. But, like I said, the Black Mariahs are powerful here."

I could feel my heart start to beat faster. "Yes, but you said your 'father'?"

"Sorry, I'm so used to people knowing who I am. I probably should have explained better when I introduced myself. I'm the son of General Castillo."

❧ 10 ❧

Super Doll

It took a moment for his words to truly sink in. *He was the general's son?*

"I'm embarrassed," Julian said. "I should not have expected you would know us. My father has governed the island since—"

"I know who he is." I looked down at my hands, which were now clenched together in my lap. How depressing, I thought. I meet the first person on the island I feel remotely connected to, and he turns out to be the son of the general.

Julian was smiling. "Oh, good, you've heard of him then. Well, don't believe the bad parts. He has done so much for this island, but some Carabajelians refuse to recognize it."

It occurred to me before either one of us spoke again that I should just ask him why I was giving the Carabajelians such a fright. I sat up straighter, but I struggled to find the words. He had already explained the mystery of the nun. I didn't know how to bring up the mystifying behavior of Clara, Pilar, and the other locals without sounding like a total lunatic.

Then I had an idea. Maybe I didn't have to ask him questions outright. Maybe I could get him to fess up by playing innocent. I turned to face him and forced a broad smile. "I haven't heard anything bad about him," I said. "Quite the opposite."

"I'm so glad. I can't say I always get along with the guy, but he saved this place from financial ruin years ago. Before I was born."

"The proceeds from the black sugar?" I asked.

"Right. Very good. And here I thought it was difficult to conduct any research on the island."

"I didn't research it. Actually, your father told me."

"You met my father?" His voice was incredulous.

"Yes. He invited me over for coffee yesterday because I won a scholarship to study here for the summer."

Julian's eyes opened wide. "Let me get this straight. You won a scholarship to come here, and *my father* invited you for coffee to congratulate you?"

"Or tea."

"What!"

"Yes. He invited me for coffee or tea."

Julian frowned. "What he offered you for a beverage is not the point here."

"I know, I'm sorry. I was joking. Not about your father. He did in fact invite me over."

"I'm sorry to be so surprised," Julian said, shaking his head. "You must understand how out of character that is for him."

"The Institute said something about a fundraising opportunity."

He nodded as though he agreed, but I could tell he was still stunned. "My father is just not a person one would call sociable."

"Your house is sure nice," I said, even though the word "house" didn't exactly do the palace-chateau justice.

"Yeah, quite a place. I don't live in it much, though. There are too many servants hanging around, not to mention it's bloody freezing up there most of the time. That's why I keep my room here."

"Your father doesn't mind that you want to become a doctor? I mean, don't you have to study leadership or something?"

"To rule Carabajel someday?"

"Yeah, I guess."

"Hopefully my father isn't going anywhere anytime soon. He would have preferred I studied business or law, yes, but being a doctor is what I have always wanted to do. I figure—what is the expression? The one about jumping from a bridge?"

It took me a minute to figure out what he was talking about, and then I giggled. "Not jumping. Crossing. Crossing a bridge when you come to it. Though maybe in your case, you will have to jump."

He laughed and put his arm around me. My tummy fluttered ever so slightly when he touched me, and the sensation annoyed me. I didn't want to like this guy.

"I'm glad I met you, Piper," he said. "This has been a highly entertaining Sunday."

"For me too. I'm sorry again for attacking you. I'd have thought the son of the general would have bodyguards or something."

"My father would like nothing more than to have me followed constantly, but he settled for letting me drive a really fast car. Besides, I don't think he ever expected my biggest threat would be in the school library."

I smirked. "True. But I am sorry. For all the trouble."

"Don't mention it. The whole thing is rather hilarious when you think about it. This entire campus is almost totally empty, and you and I pick the exact same time to visit the library."

He let go of my shoulder, looked at his watch, and then stood up. "Next time I will make sure I wear a little sheep's bell so you can hear me coming."

"Sounds good," I said.

"Listen, I've got to get going, but are you sure you

are feeling better? I can walk you back to your dorm if you'd like."

"No, I'm fine now. I'm totally good. Thanks."

I did feel better, except for the fact that a small part of me didn't want him to walk away. Something about his presence was comforting.

"Are you absolutely certain?"

He was looking at me with a concerned expression, but I nodded brightly. "I'm going to take a swim in the pool."

"All right, well, I'll see you around. And next time, Super Doll, take it easy on poor guys like me." He reached into his shirt pocket for his cigarettes and lighter. He offered one to me, but I shook my head. Then he winked at me and headed in the direction of his dormitory.

I watched him until he vanished behind a hedge of hibiscuses. I wondered if he'd forgotten all about the book he'd wanted from the library.

❧ 11 ❧

The Saints of Carabajel

The lounge chairs surrounding the saltwater pool were empty, and my classmates were nowhere in sight. I must say I was relieved. I wanted to go swimming undisturbed, to feel the cool water rush all around me and erase my anxiety and fanciful notions about the island.

I also wanted to forget meeting Julian. Even on the short walk from the library to the pool, I'd started replaying every single word he said, as though we'd been two actors in a stage play. *Super Doll.* What an expression.

But I winced with embarrassment about breaking down in tears. *Me, cry?* It was unheard of.

I prided myself on never crying, on being as stoic as

my dad like the Air Force ingrained. *Integrity first. Service before self. Excellence in all we do.* I had grown up under those mottos. My dad drilled them into my head as though they were multiplication tables.

I settled into the lounge chair farthest away from where the sea washed over the rocks into the pool because I wanted to read the *Saints of Carabajel* without getting soaked with spray from the waves. The cover was made from dark-brown cloth, and the title was embossed with gold ink above an ornate cross inter-twined with a sword. The author's name was at the bottom in a small font. Lucinda La Barca.

I opened the book and searched for an author's biography, but there was nothing in the front or the back. There wasn't even an acknowledgment page or a prologue or any other explanation as to why this person tackled the subject of the saints of Carabajel.

I flipped through the first half of the book, but there was very little text. There were only photographs of the saints and small captions explaining their contri-bution to life. Santa Alondra, Patron of the Children, Santa Dallendra, Guardian of the Seas, and so on.

It was not until I reached the last section of the book that I found a somewhat interesting paragraph. The author wrote: "Dysentery had wracked the island two decades before, and the Black Mariahs were the ones to come up with a cure by using a medicinal herb found in the island's volcanic ash." I wondered why

Julian had not mentioned that little tidbit of pertinent island history.

I skipped ahead to the conclusion. In one damning sentence, the book explained the Castillo family had once been the head of the Black Mariahs' guard unit until the nuns discovered the black sugar. The general and his men wanted to control the sugar trade, so they overthrew the nuns and set up their own military regime.

I yawned. It sounded pretty commonplace to me. It was even a little boring. *A religious order miraculously saves the people from disease and then a new leader takes over and manages to incense everyone in his path, despite making the locals prosperous.* I put the book down on the little cocktail table next to my chair.

I must have dozed off in the sun because the next thing I heard was a squeaky girl's voice saying, "Piper? Piper? Are you asleep?"

I opened my eyes and even with the glare from the sun, I could see it was Coco standing over me wearing the silliest bathing suit I had ever seen, especially for someone who was concerned about the sun. Her white bikini top was connected to her bottom piece by gold hoops around her waist.

"What's so funny?" she asked when she saw my expression.

"Coco, I'm sorry, but where did you get that bathing suit?"

"L.A. Do you like it?" She sat down in the lounge chair next to me.

"It's not exactly my style, as I'm sure you can tell." I motioned to my own simple, black one-piece.

"Like I said, my fashion is my art."

"How could I forget?" I replied. I had to admit, I admired someone who spoke with such conviction.

"Am I bothering you? I wanted to come down to the pool, but I didn't want to go by myself and everyone else went downtown. Then I saw you from my balcony."

"It isn't bad to do things alone sometimes, you know."

"But I can't swim, so if I fell in no one would be there to help me."

"You're from California and you can't swim?"

"No way. Not with those waves and sharks."

"What makes you think I can save you?"

"I don't know. You seem self-sufficient."

I shrugged and stared out at the ocean. It looked so flat from where we sat, but the rollers were starting to crash on the seawall with rising force.

"What are you reading?" Coco asked after a while. She picked up my library book and started leafing through it.

"A book on the island. Nothing interesting," I said. "I needed a break from Spanish."

"Me too. I was wondering, Piper, have you given any thought to my essay?"

"Not really," I admitted. "Look, Coco, I'd love to help, but we're so busy with work here."

"I'll pay you five hundred dollars. Cash."

I couldn't believe she was serious. "To help you?" I asked. "Or to write it for you?"

"To help me. I know you think the topic is stupid, but I can make it more interesting. I can talk about how couture fashion is expressionism too."

"I don't think it's stupid, Coco. It's just not my world. Fashion and art and Paris and all that."

Coco frowned. "You know, Piper, you think you are so much smarter than everyone else—and maybe you are—but you don't have to act that way all the time."

Her comment took me aback. "I don't think I'm smarter than you, Coco," I said quietly. "I'm telling you I doubt my skills in this particular area."

She slumped in her lounge chair and held my book high in the air so I couldn't see her face. After a few minutes, she said in a little girl voice, "But you'll still help me?"

"Yes, I will help you." I wanted to ask for my book back, but she was so engrossed in it, I felt bad taking it away from her.

I reached into my bag and dug out Becky's journal and my pen. *Day thirteen*, I wrote at the top. *This island is the strangest place I have ever set foot on.* I had nothing else to add since I hadn't solved any of the mysteries I'd set out to solve, so I settled for working on my Spanish translation homework.

Coco and I stayed at the pool until the late afternoon sun began to wane. "I'm starving," she said. "Do you want to have dinner with me downtown?"

I was about to automatically decline, but I stopped myself before shaking my head. I was hungry, and suddenly, I felt like I could use a few hours off campus and away from my ever-lingering thoughts about generals and nuns and now Julian.

"That sounds good," I replied. "I'm hungry too. But nothing too fancy, okay? I'm the scholarship student, remember?"

She looked embarrassed until I laughed.

"We'll walk there and go to a little café or something, I promise," she said.

We gathered up our things and set off for the dormitory. She was still holding on to my book and didn't mention it until we reached my door.

"I'll meet you downstairs in twenty minutes," she said. "Here's your book. Sorry I commandeered it all afternoon. It was really fascinating."

"It was?" I asked, surprised.

"I couldn't figure it out. It's all about saints, but not a single one of those people are real saints."

"I don't get it."

Coco shrugged and started to walk down the hall toward her room.

"Wait," I called after her. "The saints aren't real?"

She whirled around and walked backward as she spoke. "Nope, not a single one of them."

"How do you know?" I asked, but she was already skipping away.

"I went to Catholic school for twelve years," she said over her shoulder.

12

The Rosary

I stood in the hallway, staring after her retreating figure until she reached the door to her room and opened it. Then I closed my own door, sat down on my bed, and leafed through the book again. The people in the photographs were definitely real human beings. And they certainly looked like they could have been saints. Their faces were plastered with thoughtful, angelic expressions as though they were pondering a pathway to the heavens or something.

I looked closer at the page, thinking maybe it would betray a clue, but even at two inches away from my face, I couldn't see anything different. I wasn't sure what a real saint looked like, but the figures in the book definitely gave off a holier-than-thou vibe.

I tossed the book onto my desk and went into the bathroom to take a shower. I stood with my head bent down and let the hot water soothe the back of my neck. I started to feel the first inkling of a headache coming on, and for a few moments, I considered canceling with Coco. After the long day, I wanted nothing more than to climb into bed.

But what if I run into Julian again downtown? I quickly reprimanded myself. *Don't be stupid. You don't even know the guy. He probably has girls crawling all over him.*

Besides, I had more important matters to attend to. I had to interrogate Coco about the book and the saints not being saints.

When I got out of the shower, I rummaged through my makeup bag looking for the aspirin bottle Becky had insisted I bring along. I swallowed two of the little pink pills and prayed they would kick in before a serious migraine started.

Coco was waiting for me in the lobby. She was actually wearing jeans for once. But then I sighed. She had rolled them up at her ankles to show off silver stilettos.

"Coco, are you sure you can walk all the way to town in those?" I asked.

"We'll find out. I can always take them off."

I felt like asking why she would go through the trouble to wear such dressy shoes if she was just going to end up barefoot, but I held my tongue.

"Have you seen any of the others?" Coco asked. "I

can't believe they've been gone all day. I even knocked on a few of their doors to see if they wanted to come with us, but no one answered."

I looked around the lobby. There was no sign of anyone except Pilar, who was filing something away in a cabinet at the far end of the room.

"Did you ask Pilar? Maybe they mentioned something to her."

"No, good idea. Pilar?" Coco called. "Pilar?"

Pilar turned around slowly, and I saw that she wasn't Pilar after all. She was a new housekeeper. One I had not seen before.

"I'm so sorry," Coco said. "I thought you were Pilar. Have you seen the others in our group?"

The woman didn't answer right away. She turned her gaze on me, and I instantly got the same uneasy feeling I had gotten with Clara. But to my surprise, her face registered zero emotion.

"Do you speak English?" Coco asked.

"Yes, of course," the housekeeper replied. "But I have not seen any of your friends."

"Okay, gracias," Coco said, but the housekeeper barely acknowledged her. She just stared at us with a plastic smile.

Coco pulled me by the elbow. "Come on, maybe we'll find everyone downtown. They must still be there."

"Was it me, or was the new housekeeper acting

weird?" I asked, but Coco shrugged in her noncommittal way.

"This whole place is spooky if you ask me. And I keep hearing bells that keep me up half the night."

"They're from a convent. It's somewhere around here, but I haven't seen it."

"Well, the sound is making me go batty."

"I get it," I replied. I was glad at least I wasn't the only one getting all creeped out by the place.

We had walked about a mile outside the gates of the campus when suddenly, without thinking, I turned right and led us down a narrow cobblestone side street.

"Where are you going?" Coco asked.

I stopped walking. *Where had I been going?* Ahead of us farther up the lane were the ruins of a Gothic church. It had arched windows and a high tower in the front above the door. Some of the windows were empty shells while others were boarded up and covered with black flowers and vines. A different image of the church floated through my mind. Instead of being abandoned, its front door was open, and women wearing long black robes and veils were hurrying up the front stairs. I gulped.

"Piper?"

"I believe this is a shortcut," I said, trying to keep my voice steady.

"Thank goodness. I need a shortcut. My feet hurt already."

But was it a shortcut? I wasn't entirely sure. I had a horrible feeling if I kept walking toward the church, the road would veer to the left and lead to a stone staircase that would bring us right down to the walled city.

I took a few tentative steps forward and Coco followed me. Part of me wanted the staircase to be there. The other part of me feared it was indeed going to be there.

"How did you figure this way out?" Coco asked.

"I looked at a map," I said quickly.

"Beyond."

"Right, beyond."

We passed in front of two connected stucco townhouses that also looked empty and approached the church. I swallowed hard.

Behind the thick greenery of the abandoned church was a wrought iron banister. A lone gaslight flickered above it, marking the first step. We pushed the vines aside, and I stepped down onto the first step and then stopped. I had been on those steps before. *But when? And how?*

"What's the matter?" Coco asked. "Is it slippery? I see a lot of moss."

I looked down and she was right. A layer of moss covered the surface like a carpet.

"Yeah, it is slippery," I replied. I reached for the cold bannister and Coco did the same. The closer we got to the bottom, the more the inexplicable vision faded away. Thankfully, Coco started chattering about nothing in particular, so I just nodded and said "hmm" until we reached Carabajel's main street, the Avenida Lourdes.

We stopped at the first casual-looking restaurant we found, a small place called Café Maya with outdoor tables and chairs facing the road so we could watch the passersby. A waiter came over and handed us menus, and we both decided on fried shrimp and rum and pineapple juice since nothing even remotely indicated a drinking age on the island.

I waited before I questioned her about the book. Sitting there in the fading sun felt nice, and I had to admit, I was having a good time hanging out with her. Once I got past the outrageous clothes and the fashion essay talk, she was actually sweet and funny. But even as we talked about class and how Cecilia was overly cheery one day and then seemingly hungover the next, my mind kept drifting back to the Gothic church and how I'd had an epiphany the staircase was there.

The whole episode was like the déjà vu I'd experienced when I first landed on the island. There had been something so familiar about the gnarled tree, I had been certain there was a cemetery beyond it. But there wasn't one. *Or had there been?*

I wondered if I should go back to the airport and look again. *Maybe I had missed it. But what would it prove? That I was losing my mind?*

I forced myself to stay focused. I still had to ask Coco more about the saints in the book.

"Coco," I finally began, and then took a bite of shrimp. "I'm going to read the saint book when we get back to the dorm. What were you saying earlier about them not being real?"

Coco looked bored. "I don't know. Whoever wrote it was clearly an idiot. The author made a big deal about the saints the nuns here worship, but none of those saints were real people."

"But how are they not real?"

"Don't you know what a saint is? They were living people the church canonized because they did something amazing. But none of the people in the book are saints."

"But how do you know?" I pressed her. I wasn't sure what I was getting at, but I also wasn't sure why someone would have written a history book about the island and put fake saints in it. No wonder Julian had called it trash.

"I told you I went to Catholic school my entire life, and all my nannies were Catholic. Believe me, I practically had to memorize every saint out there, and not one of them is in the book."

"Maybe they aren't Catholic saints. Maybe these nuns aren't even Catholic," I offered.

But Coco shook her head. "No, they are. The book

says they are. I think the author must have gotten confused or didn't do her homework."

"And that's the only explanation?" I asked.

"It was probably a student's dissertation or something."

"So strange."

"Totally."

I turned my attention back to the street. The vendors were beginning to set up their tables and food carts for the evening's celebration, or rebellion, or whatever it was.

Way off in the distance, I could see the silhouette of two Black Mariahs walking together in the middle of the road. They each carried an overflowing basket filled with black hibiscuses. I cast my eyes downward, but still, I was certain I could feel them looking at me with long, fixed stares.

WHEN WE RETURNED FROM DINNER, ALL OF OUR classmates were seated around the small pool outside the lobby, talking and laughing loudly.

"There they are!" Coco said.

We walked over and sat down in the empty seats between Gareth and Gemma.

"Where have you two been?" Gemma purred.

"We went out to dinner at some café," I replied.

"Café Maya. We got shrimp," Coco added. "What about you?"

"We went shopping all day. Aisling's fault," Kimberlee said, and Aisling smiled. She was stretched out on the lounge chair like an elongated cat.

"I was their valet," Gareth said. "I carried the bags."

Pathetic, I thought and rolled my eyes.

"Coco, you should have joined us. And you, Piper," Sofia said.

Before I could thank her for including me, Aisling leaned forward and said in a mock drawl, "Soooo, Piper, who is the guy who was looking for you?"

Everyone except Coco laughed hysterically.

"What guy?" I asked evenly, though of course I knew.

"You tell us," Aisling said and crossed her arms.

"I have absolutely no idea."

"Come on, Piper. You are not really telling us a hot guy shows up out of nowhere, asks what your room number is, and you have no idea who he is," Aisling said.

"I'm just surprised, that's all," I replied.

I guessed that Julian must have come back after Coco and I left for Carabajel. And I chided myself for feeling slightly excited. He was probably just checking up on me after my panic attack in the library.

I realized all eyes were still on me. "Okay, fine, I did meet one of the college students in the library. It must have been him."

"I thought all the students were gone," Gareth said. "And why were you in the library?"

I ignored the question. "They are all gone except for him." I was about to mention he was the general's son, but I stopped myself. *Why, I don't know.* I felt like I was giving away a state secret or something. "This guy had special permission to stay here," I said. "Don't ask me how."

"He was something," Aisling said. "Lucky you." She made a face as though she was terribly surprised a good-looking guy was interested in me.

"Did you give him my room number?" I asked.

"Of course. I wasn't going to let you miss an opportunity like him."

"Thanks," I murmured. I wanted to hurry up to my room to see if he'd left me a note, but I didn't want to appear desperate. Instead I leaned back against my chair, stared up at the stars, and pretended not to care.

I had to admit, the stars were pretty extraordinary like the planetarium guy had said. They looked even more prominent over the sea than they did over the desert out west.

I sat with the group for another twenty minutes or so until the conversation turned to other gossip. Gemma and Bronwyn started talking about things they bought for Smith, Gareth cuddled up to Aisling, and Coco got into a heated debate with Sofia about whether or not Vail or Aspen could compete with Gstaad and Chamonix.

I finally yawned, stood up, and said good night to everyone.

"See you in the morning. Buonanotte!" Gemma said.

"That's Italian," Gareth corrected.

"Like I care about Spanish," Gemma said.

I shook my head. I was definitely ready to be rid of them for the night.

As soon as I turned the corner on the other side of the lobby, I almost ran up the stairs to my room. But there was nothing there. No note, no message, nothing. I even opened and closed the door twice to make sure nothing got stuck under it.

Stupid to be acting this way, I thought as I fastened the latch.

I was bone-tired, so I stumbled around looking for something to use as pajamas. Barely awake, I brushed my teeth and then fell into my bed in a merciful, dreamless sleep.

My last thought was that I missed my dad. *He'd enjoy my stories about this nuthouse of an island.*

I WOKE UP HOURS LATER TO USE THE BATHROOM. THE moonlight had diminished, and my room was pitch black.

I shuffled in the dark and turned sleepily, bumping into the edge of the sink. Mentally, I cringed and waited for the sound of my makeup bag crashing onto the bathroom floor. My bathroom was small, so the only place to put the thing was on the edge of the counter right where I would be sure to knock it off every time I walked in. But instead of feeling my elbow connect with the bag, I was met with empty air. Confused, I flipped on the light switch.

My makeup bag was nowhere to be found.

I looked around the edge of the toilet and even under the sink. It had to be there. I never moved the bag out of the bathroom. I backed away and turned on all the lights in the room. Every light. Even the little nightlight next to my bed. I opened the closet. I checked under the bed.

I tried to recall my evening. I had been at the pool with Coco. I'd come back to my room, showered, and put on makeup. I took two aspirin because I had a headache. Then I put the bag back in its place on the counter.

I turned in a full circle and threw up my hands in frustration. And then I spotted it sitting on top of my desk in a place I was certain I'd never put it before.

I emptied it out, but nothing appeared to be missing. It made no sense. *Who would break into some girl's dorm room for the sole purpose of moving her mascara and lipstick to another location?*

Maybe it was the new housekeeper, I reasoned. Pilar had the day off and perhaps the new woman did a turn-down service. Why she didn't make my unmade bed I couldn't explain, but nothing else was out of order. It was the only logical explanation.

After my latest self-inflicted scare, I was too jittery to sleep. I tossed and turned with the lights on for about a half hour before giving up and reaching for the book on the saints. I checked the index again for anything resembling what Clara had whispered when she gave me the rosary. Santarella. Santa Rella. *What else did it sound like? Santa Ella?* Even trying different pronunciations did not turn anything up.

I decided to inspect the rosary again for lack of any other options, thinking maybe I had missed an inscription. I leaned over and slid open the nightstand drawer where I had stashed the rosary. I reached in and moved my hand across the bottom of the drawer, but I couldn't feel it. I yanked the drawer open.

But it wasn't there.

I shook the drawer. I pulled it out entirely and turned it upside down. No rosary. And then I looked up and gasped. I had no idea how I missed it earlier.

The rosary was hanging on the wall above my bed.

13

Finding the Convent

The one positive about not going back to sleep was I was the first person down for breakfast the next morning, which was good because I wanted to speak with the new housekeeper privately. I had two missions to accomplish. First, I had to get to the bottom of who was in my room. Second, I really, really needed to call my dad.

I had come to one logical conclusion—someone had entered my room while I was out to dinner with Coco, discovered the rosary, and then hung it up on the wall. That same person may or may not have moved my makeup.

I was reasonably sure even if Julian had knocked on my door, he would not have broken in, relocated my makeup bag, and hung up a rosary. That left the house-keeper. *But why? Was she having a slow night? Or was she trying to tell me the same thing Clara was trying to say to me? Something about a Carabajel saint? And why on earth did it involve me?*

The lobby was empty, but the table outside the door to the Reef Room was already set up with pastries, coffee, and croissants. I grabbed a guava pastry and gobbled it down as I headed for the dilapidated pay phone. I picked up the receiver and heard the loud hissing noise again. I pressed zero and waited to see if anything would happen this time. Seconds later, a female voice said—or rather shouted—something in rapid Spanish.

"I need to call the United States," I tried, hoping I was speaking with an operator. "Estados Unidos?"

"Numero?" she asked.

I rattled off our New Jersey number and then she barked, "Nombre!"

"Piper."

There was a loud click, and then I actually heard ringing and the blessed sound of my father's voice saying hello.

"Llamada por cobrar desde Piper," the operator said.

I don't know how much he understood, but he caught my name and said, "I accept the charges." There was another loud click.

"Dad, Dad?"

"Piper! Finally. How's it going down there?"

I had no idea if the scary operator was still on the line, and I didn't care. What I wanted to say was, "This place is a cluster. Get me off on the next flight," but Julian crossed my mind and I stopped myself. "It's good, Dad. It's all good."

"I was getting worried."

"I'm sorry it took so long to call you. There is only one phone in this whole place, and it has been broken."

"I assumed as much. I called the Institute headquarters a few days ago and told them telecommunications there were shot. But they assured me you were fine."

"You called about me? Gosh, sorry."

"No problem. Becky has been asking every day if I heard from you. Is it paradise or what? You learning anything?"

"I am learning, really I am. And the island is incredibly beautiful. They have this black sugar and these trippy nuns hanging around, and the general of the whole island had me over for coffee in his palace because I won the essay contest."

"The general had you over for coffee? You're in the big leagues now, kid."

"That's one way to put it."

There were so many other things I wanted to tell him. How rich the other kids were, how the general's behavior pointed to an ulterior motive beyond a tea party, how the nun looked at me on the beach like she recognized me, how I met Julian in the library and almost knocked him out, how his father's housekeeper had shoved a rosary into my palms, how someone else moved my things around and had even gone so far as to nail the rosary to my bedroom wall, and how there was a history book about the island with saints in it who weren't really saints.

Instead, I said nothing. I was too afraid the telephone was going to drop the call in the middle of the story and panic him. I knew he'd be so concerned he would probably send a U.S. Air Force plane to get me.

"Six more weeks to go," my dad said. "Are you sure there's no email?"

"I wish."

"Unbelievable. Anyway, you need to keep an eye on the weather. It's hurricane season, remember? There is a storm out there getting worse."

"I will, I promise."

"And be sure to listen to the Institute's instructions and don't do anything stupid, okay?"

"You got it."

I heard a rustling behind me, so I balanced the receiver against my shoulder and turned around. Pilar was leaning over the breakfast buffet, straightening out a stack of napkins I most likely knocked over. As much as I wanted to keep talking to my dad, I also wanted to question Pilar before everyone else showed up.

"Anyway, Dad, I'm sure this is costing a fortune, so I better hang up."

"Call me again when you can, Pipes. Or if you need anything."

I hung the phone up and felt a nauseating pang of homesickness, and I gulped to tamp it down.

"Pilar?" I called out.

When she saw it was me, she put down the napkins and stood immobile, her hands at her sides. "Si, señorita?" she asked.

I lowered my voice as I got closer. "Pilar, I have a question. The new housekeeper, I think she moved some things around in my room and I want to ask her about it. Do you know where I can find her?"

"New housekeeper?"

"Yes. I'm not angry. I just want to speak to her for a moment."

Pilar shook her head.

Maybe I wasn't explaining myself properly. I tried again. "Okay, maybe she's not new, but I am talking about the housekeeper who replaced you yesterday."

"No, no. Lo siento," she said.

"Pilar," I whispered, "I swear, there is no problem here. I only want to talk to her for a second to ask her a question."

Pilar crossed her arms and took a step back from me as though I were threatening her. "No new housekeeper, señorita. We all had vacaciones. Vacation. No one was working ayer. Yesterday."

FOR THE REST OF THE DAY, I SAT AT MY DESK AND didn't speak to anyone. I felt majorly defeated and completely bewildered. I was relieved Cecilia did not have any interactive lessons planned. Instead, we each had to translate two pages of Carabajel's Spanish-language newspaper, *El Diario*, and then write an essay about intercultural communication.

I wished my particular article had been interesting because it would have taken my mind off everything, but instead my assignment was dull. People were complaining the new traffic pattern around the airport was causing congestion. Boring.

I wondered for the thousandth time if I should tell Cecilia someone had been in my room and was also possibly posing as a housekeeper. But the last part was ludicrous. Pilar must have been wrong. Someone had been working yesterday. I had seen her with my own eyes and so had Coco. And she had been wearing the same uniform as Pilar. She had even been going through the filing cabinet.

I put my pen down and looked out the window. Beyond the palm trees surrounding our building, I could see the path to the library. Suddenly I knew what I had to do. I had to find Julian and somehow get him to either bring me back to the palace so I could question Clara or explain things himself.

When class finished at five o'clock, I hurried back to my room before anyone asked what I was doing for dinner. I had taken special care to make a mental note of where I left everything to see if anything was out of order. I checked the location of my makeup bag, my overnight bag, and the pile of clothes I had intentionally left on my bed, but nothing had been moved.

I dropped my book bag on the chair and hid my wallet between the mattress and the box spring. If I located Julian, I wanted to give the impression I was out for a casual walk so the only thing I brought with me was my lip gloss.

And then what, Piper? I asked myself. Are you going to say, "Can I go to your dad's house again?"

Admittedly, my plan was a little foolish, but at least it was a start.

I locked my door and went down the staircase as quickly as I could. I caught a glimpse of everyone sitting around the pool with plates from the dinner buffet, so I ducked around the other side of the building and took the outer path by the saltwater pool and the seawall where I had sat with Julian. When I reached the library, it was dark inside. I tried to open the front and side doors, but this time they were locked.

I walked over to Julian's dorm, but it was shuttered

too. Every single curtain was drawn tightly, and every balcony door was closed. Even the parking lot was deserted. I couldn't believe Julian was staying in the dormitory all by himself.

And then I heard the bells.

I tilted my head toward the sound. From what I could tell, there was no tune being played. It was only the sound of bells, ringing again and again and again. *Spooky*. Like Coco had said.

I shaded my eyes to look at the sun. Even with the ever-present clouds, I could see it was still high in the sky. I estimated I had at least two hours of daylight left. I wondered if it would be crazy of me to take a walk along the beach and try to find the convent. Yes, it would probably be absolutely insane, I reckoned.

I quickly weighed my other options. I could go back to the dorm and sit in my room. I could go back to the dorm and work on Coco's essay. I could go back to the dorm and relax at the pool with everyone. None of the options were particularly appealing to me, even if I was getting hungry.

I was also overcome by a sudden urge to see the mystery convent for myself. For whatever reason— maybe because of the way the Black Mariah looked at me or maybe because of Julian's ominous warning to stay away—my curiosity was piqued.

I'll just walk along the beach for a while and see

what is there, I told myself. No big deal. A simple walk on the beach.

I assessed the thick brush covering the entire mountainside. It was hard to believe there was anything up there besides an endless jungle.

I set off toward the seawall. I decided I would take the same path I'd followed the first day of class when I saw the Black Mariah on the atoll, only this time I would stay close to the underbrush lining the shore. In case there were any nuns out for their daily exercise routine, I wanted to spot them before they spotted me.

When I reached the stream, I crossed it by jumping from rock to rock. When I was safely on the other side, I ever so slowly crept the rest of the way down the path to the black sand beach. I pushed myself up against the thickest mangrove bush I could find and looked in both directions. Except for a few straggly looking ocean birds, the beach was empty as far as my eyes could see.

The sight was so breathtaking I momentarily forgot my entire plan and stood there transfixed by the beauty of the view in front of me. It was inexplicable how a place so spectacular could be so creepy. I had to remind myself to keep moving unless I wanted to risk running out of daylight.

I clung to the water's edge for about a half mile, looking behind me every so often to make sure no one was following me. The farther I got from campus, the narrower the beach became so in some places, the incoming waves almost went far enough across the sand to touch the underbrush. I either had to try to run forward ahead of the sea or push myself into the thicket to keep my feet from getting wet. I prayed the tide was going out and not coming in. Otherwise, I was going to be stuck in a mangrove trap. But even that was not enough to stop me from pushing on.

"There is no way I'm going back until I see this convent," I said under my breath. Something was driving me forward, and I didn't know what it was.

I checked the sun's position. There was more cloud cover than there had been earlier, but I could still see the sun peeking out. I knew I had better get a move on. Seeing the convent in the daylight was one thing. Seeing it at night was an entirely different story.

As I walked along, I tried to find the convent's path into the rainforest, but the foliage was so dense it was impenetrable unless one happened to be taking a stroll with a machete.

I wondered why anyone, even nuns, would ever choose to live so remotely. Going out for a gallon of milk had to be a major excursion. Looking up at the cliff of a mountain alongside me, I couldn't imagine there was even a way to get a car up there.

I kept walking in the soft black sand until the end of the beach came into view and curved out toward the sea. In front of me was a spiral staircase leading up a stone barrier. Both were nearly hidden by an overgrown privet hedge and sea heather.

I climbed the steps slowly and stood at the top, momentarily baffled. To my left was the sea, and to my right was the wall of mangroves. I didn't see a gate or a door, but the staircase had to lead somewhere.

I reached out and shook the sea heather a little and, sure enough, there it was. Buried in the hedge was a gate about two feet taller than me. I expected it would be locked, but when I pushed it, it flew open on its hinges. I cringed and wished I had tried a gentler approach. I had a sudden vision of a group of nuns standing on the other side, watching my grand entrance. But I took a deep breath and took one step forward anyway.

I found myself staring at a crescent-shaped cove surrounded on all sides by mountains. A pier stretched far out into the black sea, and at the very end was a torch that flickered with high flames.

I had to grasp a clump of sea heather to keep myself from tripping over the threshold of the gate. Without a doubt, it was impossibly and inexplicably the scene from my dream.

When I regained my footing, I had a sudden, horrid feeling someone was watching me. But when I looked over my shoulder, the beach behind me was still empty. The only thing different was that even in just the few moments I'd been standing there, the waves had calmed down. Instead of crashing on the beach, they were now sliding across the sand, gently and silently.

My dream had been fuzzy, but the scene before me was unmistakable, right down to the torch at the end of the pier. There had to be some explanation. Photographs I had seen online? An old book I might have leafed through at the library in Sandy Point?

I squatted down on the ledge and grasped the sea heather tighter. I leaned around the edge of the gate again and looked to my right.

There was a convent there all right. A vast, magnificent convent set back against the mountain. It was five stories tall and had a high bell tower in the center and two sharply peaked wings on either side. A stone porch with arched columns was set on the ground floor, and gaslights hung from the ceiling. At the very top of the bell tower, a cross faced the sea, blazing with light. I wished I had binoculars because I wanted to see the place up close, to glimpse inside those smoky, vacant windows.

I looked out at the sea and was surprised to catch a glimmer of movement far out past the breakers. About one hundred yards offshore, the water was parting as something moved beneath it. I squinted to try and get a better look. Whatever it was, it was heading slowly in the direction of the beach.

I still had the haunting sensation someone was watching me. I kept glancing back at the beach behind me, but nothing was there. I looked toward the convent again. I wondered if anyone could see me from the porch or the windows, but I was so deeply embedded in the sea heather, I was practically part of the bush.

The object in the water was getting closer and moving toward the shore. I held my breath and waited. Then I saw a head. It wasn't a fish after all. It was a swimmer. Someone was swimming underwater and then resurfacing every few feet for a breath of air. The swimmer was way offshore. *What about sharks? Or getting a cramp and drowning?*

The lifeguards on the ocean beach in New Jersey were always putting up colored flags to warn swimmers of offshore dangers. Red was high hazard. Yellow was a riptide warning. Purple was for dangerous marine life, which everyone knew meant a man-eating shark had been sighted.

But this beach was empty and, from what I could tell, the convent wasn't staffed with lifeguards. Whoever it was swimming, he was strong and moving fast through the water. I rechecked the sun's position. It was getting lower by the second and was starting to slip behind the clouds. I knew I should start heading back before I lost the daylight, but I desperately wanted to see who was going to come out of the water.

My legs were beginning to ache from the position I was in, so I stood up and shook them out. They were prickly with pins and needles. I scanned the surface of the water, looking for the head. For a few seconds, I didn't see anything, and then, pop, the head reappeared and disappeared again.

I held my breath. A few more strokes and the swimmer would be in the shallows. Even in the fading light, I could see where the water changed from the navy-blue color of the depths to the turquoise of the shallows.

I was right about the depth because when the swimmer reappeared, he was walking in shoulder-deep water. But as the person ambled closer to the shore, I realized it was actually a woman wearing a black bathing cap. She moved languidly in the light surf, taking her time to leave the water. When she stepped onto the beach, she reached up and pulled off her bathing cap, exposing long jet-black hair. She was also wearing a string bikini.

Well, I thought, she can't possibly be one of the Black Mariahs.

I was wrong. After she dried herself off with a black towel, she bent down again and picked something else up. I could tell before she even pulled it on that it was her habit. I almost laughed aloud. The nuns were stunning, and they wore bikinis?

A bird cawed loudly behind me and I jumped a little, not expecting it to be so close. When I looked over my shoulder, I saw it was a beautiful bird. It was large, almost the size of a seagull, but instead of being white and gray like the seagulls in New Jersey, it was a deep purple and the feathers on its belly were pink. It was walking in the sand, paying no attention to me, but it cawed again as though searching for its mate.

I turned back toward the nun. She had fastened her veil on her head and was staring directly at me, her arms crossed over her chest.

Had she seen me? I wasn't sure, but I didn't want to take any chances. It was all the bird's fault. If it had not made such a racket, she never would have looked in my direction.

She started to walk toward me at a fast clip. Julian's warning came back yet again. *They are both dangerous and not dangerous.* There was no way I was going to stick around to find out what he meant.

I scampered down the staircase and started to run. I looked over my shoulder once as I was running to be sure she wasn't chasing me, but the beach remained empty. The tide was still coming in, and this time I didn't even bother to try to avoid getting my feet wet. I ran straight through the waves, black sand and saltwater splashing up all over my clothes. I didn't know what was making me run since no one was following me, but I kept going anyway.

My mind was racing along with my body. Maybe it was playing tricks on me, but I started thinking back to the first time I had seen the essay contest poster. The photograph. It had attracted me instantly, and I finally understood why—because it had been familiar.

"That's it," I panted aloud. Forget Spanish. Forget Julian. I'm calling my dad, and he is going to get me the heck off this rock.

I was running so fast I was almost closing in on the path to the campus. I raced back across the stream and past the seawall and sprinted toward the lobby. If the pay phone is not working, I am going to smash it to pieces, I thought. I turned the corner of the octagon building and barely noticed the sleek black convertible parked across the lot from the lobby.

I swung the door open and stopped short. Julian was standing in the middle of the lobby with his back to the door, conversing with Pilar, who looked astonished Julian Castillo was standing in front of her desk. He turned around and smiled when he saw me, and then his expression changed to shock.

"Piper!" he exclaimed, rushing over to me and grasping my arm. "What happened now? Are you all right?"

I struggled to catch my breath. Pilar was watching us suspiciously, but when I looked over at her, she took off through the side door.

"Yeah, I'm okay, why?" I tried to ask casually.

"Because you don't look okay."

"No, I'm good, really!" As soon as the words came out of my mouth, I looked down at my clothes. I was filthy. My legs were splattered with wet dark sand, and my shorts were practically drenched from running through the water. I wiped my hand across my forehead sheepishly.

"I must say, I've seen you look better," Julian said.

"I was just out jogging. You know, like an impromptu-type run."

"I see, impromptu jogging, of course. I hear it is a craze sweeping America. We're in no rush at all, so take your time getting ready."

"What are you talking about?" I asked.

"Didn't you get my note from last night?"

So, he had left a note after all. My first thought was Aisling or one of the girls had fished it out from under my door, but that didn't make sense. They were the ones who had sent him to my room. *The new housekeeper again? But why would she have taken it? Hadn't she been busy enough with my makeup and the rosary?*

"I never got your note," I admitted.

"Really?" He looked disappointed. "I stopped by last night and left it under your door. Your friends were sitting by the pool, and they gave me your room number. I hope you don't mind."

"It's cool."

"I asked if you wanted to have dinner with me tonight. There is a great place downtown with flamenco music and good food. My friends and I go there a lot."

I tried to digest the words. He wanted to take me

out to dinner. I felt a jolt of excitement and then my nerves kicked in. *What would I wear? What would I talk to him about?* And I was starving. *What if I devoured everything on my plate in front of him like an animal?*

"You mean tonight?" I asked.

"Yeah, of course tonight. Why do you think I am standing here?"

"My friends told me you stopped by, but I didn't see a note. The housekeeper might have thrown it out by mistake."

"Why did you come into the lobby at this exact time then?"

"I was going to call my dad."

He looked over at the pay phone. "Does that thing still work?"

"On a good day."

"If you need to call your dad, you can use my sat phone."

I thought he said cellphone. "You have cell service! How do I get it?"

"No, not cell. Satellite service. You know, instead of towers, it picks up reception from satellites in space."

"Yeah, I know where satellites are." The second I said it, I bit my lip. *Why was I always so sarcastic?* But he only burst out laughing at my response.

"Sorry," he said. "I don't know why I felt the need to explain it to you."

"It's no problem. Always good to have a refresher."

Over his shoulder, I saw a shadow move across the doorway leading to the kitchen hall. Had Pilar been listening to our entire exchange?

"What's wrong?" Julian asked.

"Nothing," I said. "I thought someone was coming."

"Do you want me to get my phone for you? It's in the car."

"No, why?"

"I thought you wanted to call your dad."

"Right, yes, I mean, no," I replied, mortification setting in. "I'll try him tomorrow."

"So, dinner then?"

"Yes. Dinner sounds great."

"Are you sure you are all right?" he asked.

"Me? Of course. I'm sorry, I'm a little distracted. I can go to dinner if you don't mind waiting while I change."

"Sure. My car is outside." He motioned across the street to the convertible.

"Okay, I'll be right down then," I said.

I dashed out the door and up the staircase to my room before he had a chance to ask why I had come running into the lobby like my pants were on fire to call home, only to forget I was making a call. I groaned in embarrassment as I unlocked my door.

I stepped inside hesitantly and looked around to see if anything had been moved, but my traps were still in place. Clothes folded neatly on the bed, comb lined up with the faucet, and rosary back in the drawer.

I caught a glimpse of myself in the full-length mirror and covered my face with my hands. I never thought I was particularly attractive, but after my escapade to the convent, I looked like a complete disaster. My dreads were sticking up all over the place, my mascara had run down my face, and I was covered in black sand. I couldn't believe he had still asked me out after taking a look at me.

I jumped in the shower, pulled my hair up in a pony-tail, and then stared at my few clothes hanging in the closet. It was going to have to be the skull dress. I yanked it over my head and slid into my other sandals.

I looked at my reflection in the mirror again. I didn't look beautiful like Coco or Aisling, or even glam-orous like the rest of the girls. The thought made me sad. But then I reminded myself that I was the one he asked out. And I was determined to enjoy the evening.

❧ 14 ❧

Flamenco Dancing

Julian was leaning against the passenger door of his car, waiting for me. He smiled when he saw me coming down the steps. "You are making quite a statement."

I looked down. "You mean the skull? What can I say? I like memento mori."

"Memento mori?"

"It means 'remember you will die,'" I said.

"You know, Piper, one of the things I like best about you is you have no problem saying whatever the hell you want."

He swung the door open for me.

"Thank you, I think."

"It's meant as a compliment." He walked around to

the driver's side, and I turned to look at him as he started the car. "Do you mean a lot of people don't speak their mind around you?" I asked.

"Only because of my father's position. Do you think I am conceited?"

"Yup."

He laughed. "See? You did it again. I can't think of any other girl who would tell me point blank I'm being conceited. What I'm trying to tell you, Piper, is I like you."

I didn't want to read into what he said, and I also didn't have time to dwell on it because Julian took the next curve so quickly, I had to grab the door handle to keep from sliding out of my seat.

"Sorry," he said. "I'll slow down."

"You do whatever works for you, but I am buckling up."

At the end of the school's driveway, he made a right turn toward downtown. We passed several cars going the opposite direction. Every single one pulled over to get out of his way as though we had a siren blaring.

"Does everyone know your car?" I asked.

"No, why?"

"Because every other car is getting right out of your way when they see you coming."

"Really? I never noticed."

We were fast approaching the rear bumper of a battered tan car in front of us. As if on cue, the driver looked into his rearview mirror and almost put his car into a ditch.

"See?" I said.

Julian slowed down, and his expression darkened. "You are very observant."

"So, they do know you?" I wasn't sure why I was pressing my point, other than it was quite obvious he was driving people off the road.

"I pretend I have a low profile, but the truth is I don't. I prefer not to focus on it. It reminds me of how abnormal my life is."

Not sure how to respond, I just looked out the window.

"Do you like flamenco music?" Julian asked as the high wall of Carabajel City came into view.

"I'm sorry, but I honestly don't know what it is."

"In that case, there is no better place to experience it for the first time than Calla Bravada."

"What is it?"

"Spanish folk music. It originated in Andalusia. It's pretty intense. Are you hungry?"

"Actually, I think I might officially be starving. Like ready to start chewing on my seatbelt starving."

"Really? Are you kidding? Aren't they feeding you enough at the school?"

"It's not the Institute's fault. I keep forgetting to eat."

"I'm glad you have an appetite then because tonight

you're going to have a fantastic dinner. The best paella anywhere on this island."

I didn't know what paella was either, but suddenly, I didn't want to seem unworldly. Something about the guy was making me want to appear at my best. It was an unusual feeling for me, and I didn't like it. I much preferred my devil-may-care attitude. It was easier. Way easier.

I took the deepest breath I could take without him noticing. Just be who you are, I told myself. If he doesn't like it, too bad.

We pulled onto Avenida Lourdes just as it was getting dark. As usual, people were walking in the direction of the street party, some carrying the candles and handbells, others pushing carts of goods. I could hear the low sound of singing in the distance. Julian was watching the spectacle and frowning.

"Not a fan of the street party?" I asked.

"It's not a party, it's a protest created by those who use religion to prey on the minds of the weak." He glanced over at me and smiled. "Let's not let it interrupt our evening," he said. "The place I'm taking you won't have anything to do with protest madness."

"What are they protesting exactly?" I asked.

"Do you really want to talk about this?"

"I'm interested."

"Protest may be the wrong word. This is one of the Black Mariah rebellions I told you about."

I looked around at the people funneling into the main square. Some were holding hands while others were singing and chanting. They seemed harmless.

"But if they're not causing a riot, then why does your father try to stop it?"

"Because he does," Julian said a little too quickly.

"Whoa," I said, backing up in my seat.

He put his hand on my knee. "I'm sorry, Piper. I don't mean to be short with you. These events haunt my father, and I take it a little personally."

He made a left turn away from the party down a narrow street lined on both sides with shuttered little shops. "Back road," he said. He looked at his watch. "Seven thirty. Good. The next show starts at eight, which will give us enough time to order dinner before it begins."

Even the mention of food was starting to make me salivate. It must have been all the running on the beach. I was so hungry I was beginning to feel cold and shaky.

But his back road did not get us too far. He made another turn, and then we came to a dead stop. The street ahead was jam-packed with traffic in both directions. Even if the drivers in front of us panicked at the sight of his car, there was nowhere they could go.

Julian shifted the car into neutral and leaned back in his seat. "Don't worry," he said. "We'll still make the show. I know exactly what this is about, and it only takes a few minutes for it to clear. We never had a problem here until the airport opened."

"To the outside world?" I teased.

"Very funny. Yes, to the outside world. Ever since Carabajel officially opened, the airport has been busy, and the cars keep backing up on the giratoria. Ah, sorry, the circulo."

It took me a minute to figure out what he was talking about, but then it clicked in.

"Oh, the rotary. I saw it when I landed."

"The rotary, yes."

"Funny, I read about it this morning in *El Diario*."

"Our esteemed local paper. Not much news, is there?"

"Small island, small news," I offered, and he smiled.

"I'm sure the article didn't mention the real reason there is a traffic problem. Our journalists are still a bit censored."

"Your father censors the news?"

"He does a bit. He wants everyone to believe they are living threat-free in a happy island paradise. He tries to portray as bright a picture as he can in the newspaper."

"To keep order?"

"In a sense, yes, though I tell him constantly everyone here is living better than they ever did before he took control. Why the Carabajelians want those irritating nuns to have power is beyond me."

I wondered if I should tell him I went to see the convent. But I wasn't sure what I would gain by telling him. Besides, I didn't want him to get angry.

The traffic inched forward, and Julian was able to make another turn down a tighter alleyway I wasn't sure was even a street. The side mirror was practically scraping the edges of the buildings on my side.

"Julian, you're pretty close on this side," I said. I didn't want him to scrape his car on account of trying to take me to dinner.

He smiled and patted my knee, and for a second or maybe two, he left his hand there, making a little ball of nerves bounce around inside me.

"Don't worry. I take this road all the time. It will get us almost to the door of the restaurant."

Up ahead, I could see figures in long black flowing robes and veiled headdresses. Even from my vantage point, I could tell they were Black Mariahs. They were holding placards above their heads, but we were too far away to see the writing on the cards.

"What's their big problem with the airport anyway?" I asked.

The *El Diario* article had made the rotary sound like a minor cause of congestion. I couldn't imagine the Black Mariahs were getting everyone all worked up over a traffic jam.

"They are upset because when we enlarged the airport, we rather unfortunately had to pave over something significant to them. I understand their problem with it, but we did move the bodies very carefully."

I felt a lump forming in my throat, and I swallowed a long, slow swallow of fear. "Wh-what bodies?"

"There used to be a cemetery right where the rotary is. And to make matters worse, their high priestess used to be buried there."

The cemetery with the white crosses. The gnarled tree. Nuns in mourning chanting a song so familiar, I could almost sing it. I thought of my mother. *Was it possible this was what happened to her? Inexplicable bouts of seeing something she was sure she had seen before, even though she knew it was physically impossible.*

Julian's face was etched with concern. "Piper, are you okay?" He picked up my left hand. I prayed it wasn't as disgustingly clammy as it felt.

"I'm sorry," I managed. "Yes, I'm okay. I think I just need to eat. I shouldn't have starved myself all day."

"Hang on, we are almost there. Maybe we should have gone someplace a little easier."

"I'll be fine, really. What did you say about a high priestess?"

"You have never heard of her? Not even in your studies?" His tone had a ring of disbelief.

"No, never."

"She was the leader of the Black Mariahs before Malfaedra. They worship her as a goddess. It's sick." He paused. "And your book? It did not explain the high priestess?"

I shook my head and held up my hands, palms open.

"You really don't know then," he said as he slid the car into a parallel parking spot and turned the engine off. He shifted toward me and ever so slightly ran his fingers gently over the top of my forehead, then down my hairline until they brushed my eyebrow. His face was so close to mine, I could feel his breath on my skin. His hand carefully pushed my chin up so he could look into my eyes. He wore a look of concern, yet something else too, something closer to longing and sadness. "Piper..." he whispered and leaned closer to me. For a second, I thought he was going to kiss me.

But he didn't.

"Don't worry about the Black Mariahs," he said. "Their time has passed."

15

Santa Vella

I tried to smile back at him, but my mind was reeling. One minute, I was stuck in horrible déjà vu and the next I was almost getting kissed by the Prince of Carabajel.

Julian stepped out of the car and came around the front to open my door. He pulled me into his arms. But only for a second. "Let's get you some dinner," he said.

He held my hand as we walked toward the door of the restaurant. We stepped into a dining room lit by silver candelabras illuminating floor-to-ceiling murals depicting Carabajel.

"Gosh, it's beautiful in here," I remarked.

"I knew you would like it."

Julian led me to a table right in front of a small stage

where two men sat tuning their guitars in front of a woman wearing a billowing yellow dress and high heels.

"The music should be starting soon," Julian said.

A host in a dark suit appeared at our table and said something to Julian in rapid Spanish to the effect of what an honor it was for us to be in his restaurant.

"Gracias, gracias," Julian replied and shook the man's hand. The man turned to me, but when he did, his eyes widened in shock, and whatever words he was about to say died on his lips.

"Antonio! Get the waiter, por favor," Julian said.

Stuttering something I didn't catch, Antonio abruptly spun on his heel and disappeared into the kitchen.

I waited for Julian to explain, but he stayed silent.

"What was that about?" I asked.

"Antonio has always been a nervous man," Julian said.

Before I could ask another question, a waiter arrived with a giant tray of food, and he began distributing it over every inch of the table. There were tiny meatballs, little sautéed clams, shrimp on skewers, cheese slices, and small balls of rice. I noticed the waiter kept his eyes down the entire time, never once glancing up at us.

"These are tapas," Julian said. "They are small plates of the house specialties. Go ahead, start eating. Do you like the music?"

"They are tuning their guitars," I said flatly.

"What? Oh yes, well, it gives you an idea of what we are in for. Did you say you had experienced flamenco before? No, you hadn't, right? This will be good. And are you enjoying the tapas?"

"Mmm, sure."

I bit into the shrimp and composed my thoughts as I swallowed. "Julian, I have to ask you something."

He winced a little before the mask of friendliness came back over his face. "You can ask me anything, Piper. But I think they are about to start playing, so why not wait until the music is over?"

"Why did the host look at me strangely? He isn't the only one, you know. This has been happening everywhere. Why?"

Julian leaned back in his chair. He looked away from me as though he wanted to say something but was trying to figure out how to word it.

I held my breath and waited for him to speak. I so badly wanted an explanation.

"I'm not sure what you mean," he finally said.

"I think you know exactly what I mean. You saw Antonio. He is not the only person to look at me as though I am the face of death. Maybe it's my hair. Are my dreadlocks against proper island etiquette or something?"

A single, long note rang out in the air, and we both looked up at the stage where a spotlight had come down on the woman in the yellow dress. She began clapping her hands, slowly at first, and then gradually building rhythm. The guitar players joined in, tapping the heels of their black boots against the wooden stage. They began playing rapidly, and the dancer swished about on stage as one of the guitar players started to sing.

"There is someone," Julian said over the music.

"What? I can't hear you."

He waved his hand in the direction of the music, indicating we would have to wait. The guitars were building to a frenzy of noise, and the dancer was spinning around the stage, her skirt flying and swishing in time to the music.

I clenched my fists in my lap impatiently. The song was endless. When it finally wound down, the crowd erupted with loud cheers.

Only Julian and I sat still and unsmiling. I waited for his answer.

"There is someone," he repeated.

"Who?"

"It is only a coincidence."

A coincidence. His father had said the same thing to me. Even the fact that I was falling for this guy was not enough for me to be able to control my rising temper.

He reached across the table, cupped my chin and looked into my eyes. "It's nothing you need to worry about."

"Nothing I need to worry about? People on this

island look at me like I have the plague, and I want to know why."

"The Carabajelians are superstitious. Can you not ignore them? There is no sense in you knowing why. It will only confuse you."

"You sound like your father," I shot at him.

My comment must have hit home because Julian looked angry. "I don't think that's quite fair," he said.

"He censors the newspapers, right, for the good of his dumb, superstitious people."

Julian's mouth turned into a hard line. "You have been here less than a month, and you dare to comment on my father's leadership?"

"No, but I have the right to know what is going on and not be treated like a child."

"If I thought you would even remotely understand what you are dealing with, I would tell you." Julian seethed as the blasted music started again.

I picked up my napkin and threw it on my plate. "Thanks for dinner and for treating me like I'm an idiot, Julian. It's been amazing." With one swift move, I pushed my chair back and stood up.

Julian reached for my hand, but I yanked it away. "Where are you going?" he asked.

"I'm leaving."

"What?"

"I'm sure none of this is your fault, but I've had it with this entire island. If you're not going to tell me what is going on, then I'll find someone else who will!"

"Piper, wait. Please."

"No way." I fumbled to pull my purse off the back of my chair. Out of the corner of my eye, I could see Antonio and our waiter staring at me from across the room with panicked expressions. I spun around in the direction of the front door.

"Wait," Julian said, but it was too late. Antonio and the waiter were already rushing toward us. As soon as they got close to me, I slid to the side and went around a table of four people, almost knocking over a bottle of white wine chilling in an ice bucket. Seeing a clear path to the door, I made a run for it. I glanced over my shoulder to see Julian trying to come after me, but Antonio and the waiter were blocking his path.

"Piper! Stop!" Julian shouted. But I didn't stop. I was so blindingly mad I didn't care what he said or wanted.

When I got outside, I took a split second to breathe in the tropical air. The street was dark and empty. I was totally disoriented, so I had no choice but to run toward the sound of the music of the religious-carnival-protest thing. I ducked down the first side street I found and dove into a high, thick hedge to catch my breath.

Standing there in the plant, my adrenaline began dropping back to its normal level. I leaned against the wall of the building behind me and sank down to the ground. I took a couple of short deep breaths. This island is officially the third circle of hell, I thought. I counted my immediate needs on one hand. I had three. I needed to get back to the campus, I needed an airline ticket off the island, and I also needed a taxi. I wasn't about to walk back to campus alone in the dark.

When enough time had passed and I was sure Julian was not going to come walking down the street, I crept out of the hedge and prayed no one had witnessed the sight of me diving into the foliage. The last thing I needed was for someone to call the local police. But much to my relief, the street was still empty, and the windows above me were dim.

At the end of the block, I came to the main thoroughfare filled with cars racing in both directions. My options for getting back to campus were limited. I could try hitchhiking, but I wasn't sure the Carabajelians would even know what a hitchhiker was, not to mention the sight of me would probably run them right off the road, thanks to whomever it was I resembled. Then to my disbelief, just as I was about to cross the street, a taxi came directly toward me. I almost cried for joy as I raised my hand to wave it over and crossed my fingers it would stop.

The cab screeched to a halt in front of me, and the driver rolled down his window. "Taxi?" he asked. Before I could answer, he yelled, "There are only two taxis in Carabajel! If I leave, you have no one. All alone! No one to get you!"

"I do, yes, I need a taxi," I said, rattled again by what was apparently the Carabajel taxi drivers' offbeat pick-up line.

But the driver was eyeing me as though I'd stuck a pin in his balloon. "You need a taxi?" he asked.

"Yes, I need a taxi!" Now I was yelling.

"Oh," he said. He slumped back in his seat. "I am a taxi."

I took a deep breath and opened the passenger door. "I know," I said. "I know you are a taxi, and I need to get to the airport."

"The airport?"

"No, I mean, I need to get to the Universidad de Villegas."

The driver looked confused. "The Universidad?"

"I have to go to both." All of a sudden, I really did need to go to the airport. I wanted to go back to the place where I had first experienced the haunting sense of déjà vu.

"Universidad first?" the driver asked.

"No, the airport first."

The interior lights of the car were on because of my open door and before I closed it again, I caught him looking at me in the rearview mirror. Here we go again, I thought. I reached into my wallet, grabbed my emergency one hundred-dollar bill, and showed it to him. "I need to get there fast," I pleaded.

He looked at the bill and nodded. "Si, si, señorita."

"Thank you."

When we arrived at the airport, I instructed the driver to pull up to the new rotary. The protesters were gone and the traffic jam had cleared, but even in the darkness I could see something was looming in the middle of the circle. It was a statue. It had been planted on the grassy mound in the center of the rotary.

"Please wait," I said as I opened the door. "I'll be right back."

The driver called something out to me as I crossed the roadway, but I didn't catch it. I sincerely hoped he would still be parked there when I got back from my little adventure, especially since I had absolutely no idea where the only other taxi on the island tended to hang out.

I crossed the road carefully and climbed over the low fence. The statue in the center was in the shape of a cross with two wings and a woman's head looking skyward, her hair tumbling over her shoulders. The statue was too high for me to exactly interpret her expression, but she was depicted either smiling, laughing, or grinning haughtily.

I knelt down and tried to read the plaque mounted at the base of the cross, but it was difficult to see it clearly. I ran my fingers across the stone, but I couldn't make out the letters, so I pulled my cell phone out of my purse. With the phone's flashlight, the writing on the stone became visible. Santa Vella, it read. And

Clara's words suddenly became clear. *Santarella. Santa Vella*.

Is that what this nonsense is about? I wondered. So, I look like the dead high priestess. What does it matter? I stomped back to the cab.

"Do I remind you of someone?" I asked.

The driver turned and looked at me, his eyes wide.

"Is it you?" he whispered.

"No. Of course not. I'm just a girl from the United States. Tell me, please. Do I look like her?"

"Y-yes, you do. Very much so."

"I do?"

"Si, señorita." He turned to face the windshield, but I could still hear his voice. "She was a legend here. She saved our people from sickness and from death. Isn't that why you wanted to stop here? To see your statue?"

"It's not my statue. This has nothing to do with me!"

"Lo siento. I'm sorry. It is the resemblance. Santa Vella has returned. This means the end is near."

"I am not Santa Vella, I promise you. And why is the end near?"

When he didn't move or respond, I held up the money again. "Please take me to the Universidad now."

He put the car in gear but tried to dig about in his glove compartment for a tissue at the same time. The car swerved to the side as he slammed the compartment closed again.

"Sorry, sorry," he muttered.

I held on for dear life as he pulled around the rotary on two wheels. Another car was already in the outer lane coming toward us, and the driver hit the horn a few times. It was an old car, rusted in places, but its windows were completely shaded. My driver was oblivious to the near crash. He blew his nose into his tissue and looked at me again in the rearview mirror. When he finally put his tissue down and grabbed the wheel with both hands, I leaned forward.

"What else can you tell me?" I asked.

"I can't, señorita, I can't."

"You can't what?"

"I have said too much already."

"Said too much about what?"

"People listen. There are observadores."

"Observers? Who are the observers?" I pressed.

"Watchers!" He turned around almost entirely in his seat to face me.

"Um, I think maybe you should watch the road."

"Si, si."

I looked out the window as we drove back through Carabajel City. *So, mystery solved.* Something about me resembled Santa Vella. *But what was the big deal? Why did everyone get so jumpy around me if she was a great leader they worshipped? And why hadn't Julian simply explained everything?*

I frowned at the last question. If Julian had been a dead ringer for George Washington and everyone in the

States kept staring at him like he had returned to the land of the living, I would at least give him the courtesy of explaining. It would have taken ten seconds for him to say, "Hey Piper, you know who you look like? The dead priestess who used to rule the island." I fumed and slouched down in the seat.

The driver accelerated, and I realized we were a few blocks away from the flamenco restaurant. I scanned the street in both directions for Julian's car, but there was no sign of it. As we came to a stop sign, I looked to our right and a car with blackened windows sat there, idling. I couldn't see the driver, but this car also looked rusty and old and very similar to the one we had cut off in the rotary. *Or was it the same car?* I looked at it more closely, but I wasn't absolutely sure.

"Why are observers watching everyone?" I asked him, but he just shook his head.

The only thing that still didn't sit well with me was the random déjà vu. But it had to be an illusion, a simple trick of the mind brought on by stress or the tropical heat.

When we finally reached the gates of the school, he slammed on the brakes so hard I fell forward, my face almost hitting the back of the seat in front of me.

"Lo siento!" he cried.

"What happened?" I looked around frantically, thinking he must have driven out of his lane again. I pushed myself back to a sitting position. At first, I couldn't see anything except the building where Cecilia lived and the octagon dormitories farther in the distance. Then I saw what had stopped him. Julian's car was parked under the lobby carport.

When Julian saw the taxi, he got out and started walking rapidly toward us. Despite myself, I was happy to see him. My anger had kind of worn off. Yes, he owed me an apology for treating me like a child who couldn't understand a simple concept, but I also owed him one for running out of the restaurant like a baby.

"The son of the general," the driver mumbled, his hands gripping the wheel.

"It's okay," I said. "He's harmless."

"The son of the general! You know him?"

"Yes, but don't worry. I'll handle him."

I tried to hand him the money, but he crumpled it and threw it back at me.

"Get out of my cab!"

"But I have to pay you something. You took me all over the island."

"Get out! Get out before he gets here!"

"I know he's the general's son, but he's not going to hurt you," I said. "Please tell me what I owe you."

"Nothing! I want nothing!"

Julian tapped on the driver's side window and motioned for him to roll it down. The driver moaned loudly and began to mumble in Spanish. Julian knocked again, and the driver pushed his forehead into the steering wheel.

Seeing the futility of the situation, I opened my door and stepped out. "He's not going to roll down the window. He's afraid of you."

"Afraid of me?" Julian shook his wallet at the glass. "He should be more afraid of not getting paid."

"It's not his fault. The man thinks you are going to haul him off to your father's dungeon."

"Dungeon? What is going on here?"

Julian knocked on the window again. "No dungeon! No voy a entrar en la dungeon!" he shouted so the driver could hear him through the glass.

"I don't think 'dungeon' is correct," I said.

"I don't know the Spanish word for dungeon."

"I thought you spoke Spanish."

"It's my second language if you want to get technical, and the word for dungeon never came up because we don't have one," he said. "Maybe if my father had a dungeon, I would've learned the correct word, and I wouldn't be standing here trying to find out how to pay this goddamn taxi driver!"

I couldn't take it any longer. I started laughing. And I couldn't stop.

"Piper," Julian said in exasperation, but I couldn't control myself. A total and complete giggle fit had taken over. Tears of laughter ran down my cheeks, and I bent over and clutched my sides in mock pain.

Julian crossed his arms over his chest, but I could tell he was trying to keep from laughing too. Shaking his head, he took a Carabajelian bill out of his wallet and handed it to me. "When you are able to breathe again please give this to the nice man who took you home?"

I took the money and held it out to the driver, but he shook his head furiously. "I give up, sir," I said. "I'm leaving it here on the back seat for you. Thank you very much for the ride." I stuck the bill under a seatbelt buckle.

The second I shut the door he revved the engine and spun out in a circle, almost crashing into the entrance gate. When his taillights disappeared into the night, I turned to face Julian. The minute our eyes met one last giggle escaped my lips.

"Are you quite through, Super Doll?" he asked.

"Yes," I said, fighting back another laugh. "Well, no. I mean, I'm really sorry. I overreacted at the restaurant. I shouldn't have run off the way I did."

"You didn't just run off! First, they tell me you went headfirst into someone's shrub, then you ended up at the airport, and the next thing I know, I get a report you are hovering around the statue on the rotary."

"I know, I was—wait, you got a report?"

"Piper, come on. My father has his men stationed everywhere. He has to on this island."

The observadores. The watchers. "You had me followed?" I asked.

"I tried to find you on my own, but you vanished. And, as far as I knew, you were miles from school with no way home. Little did I know you would manage to find the only taxi on this island."

"He's actually one of two taxis on the island."

"What? There is another one now? Well, regardless, I had no choice but to ask for some assistance locating you."

"Are you trying to tell me you were worried about me?"

"Worried about you? Not you. I was more worried about the poor people who were about to encounter you. Do you think I am going to inflict you on the locals? We would have people getting brained by books and taxi drivers having nervous breakdowns."

"Hey, the taxi driver was scared of you, not me. Why not admit you were worried about me? A little worried, maybe? A tiny bit?"

"Fine. Yes, I was worried. You took off so fast, I had no idea what to do." He grabbed my hand and began to lead me to the dormitory. "I have to say this is the most fun I have had on this island in a long time. Ever since you walked out of the pastry shop."

"So, you did see me then. Why didn't you say anything when you met me at the library?"

"I don't know. Why didn't you?"

His question gave me pause. We walked along the garden path toward the staircase, and I could hear the ocean crashing on the shore. *Why hadn't I mentioned it? Maybe I didn't want him to think he had impressed me. Or maybe I didn't want to admit to noticing him if he hadn't noticed me too.*

"I really don't know," I said.

"See? I don't know either. I was on duty when we got a call there was an impostor for Vella roaming the streets."

"Duty? You have a job?"

"I work with my father's military patrol a couple nights a week. My father thinks it is good training, so I do it to keep him happy."

"And someone called me in?"

"At first, we thought it was a joke. You know, like someone playing a prank. Then one of my father's drivers saw you too."

"Why didn't you just tell me I looked like the priestess lady? You saw Antonio's reaction to me. You were going to sit there, letting me think I was losing my mind?"

Julian stopped walking.

"What's wrong?" I asked.

"Who did tell you, Piper?"

"Who told me I look like her?"

"Yes."

Something about his voice made me feel terrible betraying the poor, sorry excuse for a taxi driver. "What difference does it make? This whole thing is ridiculous. A random person mentioned it."

"What random person?"

"Why?"

"I'm only curious."

"Someone standing at the monument."

"My father's people didn't see anyone else with you. Who was this person?"

"I don't know. If you look like the high priestess, people talk to you. Random people. You don't always get a name."

Julian shook his head. "Okay, Piper, whatever you say. I just don't want people scaring you. I want you to tell me the next time someone gives you a look. I'll make sure they won't make that mistake again."

"Let me ask you a question. If she was so wonderful, why is everyone so scared of me then? Shouldn't they be happy she's back from the dead?"

"The problem is the legend surrounding Vella has reached critical mass. Whatever."

"Whatever is right," I replied. "And why on earth did you take me to a restaurant? To panic me more?"

"It was stupid of me. I wasn't thinking. I'm really sorry."

"Forget it."

"Are we all right now?" he asked.

I nodded.

"Good."

We stayed silent the rest of the way to my room. When we reached my door, I pulled my keys out of my bag and had a thought. "Would you mind waiting so I can check my room?" I asked.

"Sure, of course. What are you checking?"

"The room scares me more than the people here."

"Why?"

"Someone went into my room while I was out, and I haven't quite got over it."

"What do you mean?"

"The other night when I went back to my room after dinner, some things were moved around."

"Couldn't it have been the housekeeper?"

"I thought of that, but when I asked the house-keeper the next day, she said no one had been working the night before. But maybe it is not a big deal because I saw a housekeeper in the office."

I was about to put my key into the lock, but Julian grabbed my arm. "Piper, this is crazy. How can you be so casual about this?"

"Because nothing was taken."

"Then what happened?"

"My makeup bag was moved."

"Your makeup bag was moved? Someone broke in and moved a bag of makeup?"

I opened my mouth to tell him about the rosary and wipe the girls-are-so-dopey look off his face, but then I thought of poor Clara. I didn't want her to get in trouble with Julian's ruthless dictator of a father.

"Yes, they moved my makeup," I replied.

"Let me get this straight. Are you telling me someone broke into your room, moved your makeup from one location to another, and then left again?"

"It sounds stupid when you say it, but that's what happened."

"I will have to put some of my father's guards on this one. We better catch this criminal before they graduate to grand theft laundry folding. This could be the start of a crime wave on this island."

"You are laughing at me."

"Yes." He snickered.

"Laugh if you want, but I maintain someone broke into my room for some reason. I don't think their sole purpose was to move my makeup. I think they were searching for something."

"All right, fine. Let's have a look around and see if anything is out of place."

I jiggled the key in the lock and opened the door.

Julian gasped. "You were right! Someone has broken in and trashed the place!"

"Don't be stupid, this is how I left it."

"Oh."

Julian went to walk around me into the room, but I blocked his way. "Wait, I have to check my traps."

"Did you say traps?"

"Yes, I set traps so I could see if anyone broke in."

"Should I be expecting a pail of water to drop on me? Or nets to fall from the ceiling? Is there a hole in the floor covered by tree branches?"

"Shut up, smartass."

Julian sat down on the bed, shaking his head as I went around checking my clothes and poking my head around the bathroom door. But everything seemed to be in order. Even the rosary was still tucked away safely in the drawer.

"Well?" he asked.

The sight of Julian sitting on my bed was worse than my scare over the rosary. I couldn't even offer him a drink, other than a half-finished diet Coke sitting on my dresser.

Julian must have sensed my nervousness because he smiled and stood up.

"It's getting late and you have class tomorrow," he said.

"You, um, don't have to go..."

"You want me to stay?"

"Yes, I mean, I'm not sure."

"A perfectly elusive Piper answer," he said.

He checked the lock on the balcony door, and then kissed me on the forehead. "You are very cute, you know. Make sure you bolt the door behind me. It's been quite a night, so you should get some rest."

I nodded meekly, relieved he was leaving and disappointed he wasn't staying longer. He walked over to the door and opened it and then turned back to me.

"I can already see going out with you is going to be a whirlwind adventure. I'll stop by tomorrow night." And, with that, he walked out.

I stared at the door for a long time afterward and tried to erase the smile from my face.

16

The Landscaper

The next morning, the first thing I did was look up Santa Vella in the library book. But as I suspected, there was nothing in it about the great island priestess. Then I inspected the inside binding and found the index page had been torn out where the "V" should have been. I flipped through the book again and, sure enough, what appeared to be an entire chapter had been very carefully knifed out.

Frustrated, I showered quickly and looked at my watch as I walked down the cement staircase. Since I had zero appetite thanks to Julian, and ten minutes before class started, I decided to try to call my dad. I wanted him to look up Santa Vella, if for no other reason than to satisfy my own curiosity.

When I walked into the lobby, Pilar passed me carrying the large coffee urn for our breakfast buffet. I gave her the biggest smile I could manage. She was her usual jumpy self at the sight of me, but for once, I could have cared less. Now that I had solved the majority of the mystery, I felt like I had the power of sanity back in my own hands.

I walked up to the pay phone, dialed zero, and braced myself for the militant sound of the long-distance operator. The phone receiver crackled, but there was no ringing and no sign of anyone at the other end. I hung up and tried again. Nothing. I tried a third time and heard a male voice say, "Operador."

"Hola? Hola?" I asked.

"Si, Operador," the voice said again.

"Llamada por cobrar. Estados Unidos?"

"Si. Numero?"

At least this guy was calmer than the last lady, I thought. I recited our number and the next thing I heard was ringing and the sound of Becky saying hello.

"Becky! Hey! It's Piper."

"Piper! Hi, sweetheart. Oh, gosh, you just missed your dad. He went to work early today. Do you want to try his cell?"

"No, that's okay. It's too hard to get a call out."

"Well, don't worry, there's nothing new here, nothing at all. How are you?"

"I'm good. Don't tell my dad, but I met a guy."

"You did?" Becky's voice went up a few octaves. "One of your classmates? Another language ambassador?"

"No, he's a student at the college here. And," I paused and lowered my voice, "you'll never believe this, but he's the general's son."

"What general?" Becky asked.

"The leader of the entire island. I didn't know it when I met him. I almost knocked him out because he crept up on me in the library by accident. Then he asked me out to dinner. And," I coughed a little, embarrassed by my own gushing, "I mean, he is a decent person."

Becky laughed. "Decent? That's it?"

"He has his moments."

"Is it safe to date the general's son? You know, being an American?"

"I don't know if his father knows or even cares. I did meet the general, though. He was a little eccentric, but his son is totally different and, like, so normal."

"Sounds exciting. Just make sure you don't fall in love and stay down there."

"Ha! There is no way I'd stay here," I said, although as the words came out, the summer suddenly felt horribly short.

"Listen, Becky, it's great talking to you, but this call will cost a fortune and my dad will kill us both. Can you do me a favor before we hang up?"

"Yes, of course."

"Would you look something up on the Internet for me really quickly?"

"Sure, let me run into the family room."

"Can you look up someone named Santa Vella? You may not be able to find anything, but I'm hoping there's a picture of her."

"Okay, no problem. I'm taking you with me," she said, meaning she was on the cordless landline we kept in the kitchen. I could hear her typing rapidly on the keyboard. "Hold on," she said, "it's coming up now. Okay, what was the name again?" she asked.

"Saint, I mean, Santa. That's the same thing. Santa Vella. V-e-l-l-a. And you should probably add Carabajel."

"All right," she said and then I heard her inhale sharply.

"What is it?" I asked.

"Piper, is this a joke?"

"No. What are you talking about?"

"A photograph of you came up."

"What?"

"It just looks like you in a nun outfit. Wow, so creepy. Who is she?"

"She was the ruler of the island years ago before she got overthrown. But I don't know much else."

"Hold on. Let me see if there's anything online."

Becky kept clicking away on the keyboard. "Okay,

here is a website that says she was the leader of an order of nuns. Oh, and wait. Apparently, there was an outbreak of dysentery years ago. Yikes, did you get vaccination shots? This Vella person came up with the cure. I wish I could send this to you. It's hysterical to see you in this getup."

There was a sharp pop on the line, and I missed what Becky said next.

"Hello? Becky? Are you there? Becky? Becky?" I slammed the receiver on the hook and cursed until I caught Pilar scowling at me.

I headed over to the buffet table and poured myself a coffee. I was loading it up with cream and sugar when Coco walked up with Gemma.

"Sooo," Coco said. "I heard you had a date last night."

I swallowed my coffee and didn't reply.

Coco nudged me. "Don't be secretive."

"I can't believe you nabbed such a hot guy," Gemma said.

"Yeah, well, whatever," I replied, feeling my face flush.

"We're teasing, Piper. We're just jealous you're having an island romance, that's all," Gemma said.

"That's right. Totally jealous," Coco added. "Now are you going to help me with my essay tonight or what? You promised."

With all the recent drama, I had actually forgotten

all about it. "Sorry, Coco," I said. "How about today right after class?"

She bit into a croissant, and a million crumbs fell down her neckline. "Oh, no! Now I'm all crumby!"

"Just shake them out," I suggested.

Coco looked disgusted. Without another word, she bolted toward the lobby door.

"Where is she going?" Gemma asked.

I sighed in exasperation. "Knowing Coco, she probably went to go take the shirt off to brush away the crumbs."

Gemma shrugged and took a sip of her coffee. She wrinkled her nose. "I thought the Caribbean was supposed to be known for good coffee."

"I'm thinking this place is known for its sugar, not its coffee."

I helped myself to a guava pastry and walked into the Reef Room with Gemma. Cecilia started class with a bang, although I was having trouble concentrating on anything she said. A nagging thought was bothering me. I kept replaying my conversation with the operator. I'd given him my phone number and he'd placed the call, but try as I might, I couldn't recall the operator determining our method of payment for the call. He didn't ask me for a credit card, nor had he asked Becky to reverse the charges. Which meant I had been allowed to place an expensive overseas phone call entirely for free. I didn't know much about pay phones, but given the keyword "pay," I highly doubted they were complimentary. Maybe I was reading into nothing, but it seemed questionable.

I was still pondering the payphone issue hours later when class finished, and I forgot all about Coco again. She caught me as I headed back to my room.

"Are you ready to help me now?" she asked. "I just need to change first."

"Right, yes, of course." I calculated quickly. It was only five o'clock. I could spend an hour or so with Coco and then still have time to hang out with Julian.

"Let's meet at the saltwater pool in a half hour," I suggested.

"Perfect. I'll be right there," she said.

After Coco bounced away, I decided to take a quick walk while she was changing so I could clear my head. I wandered in the direction of the other dorms and, as usual, the campus was deserted. The balconies were shuttered, the curtains were drawn, and there were no cars in the parking lot, except for a landscaping truck parked across from the farthest building. A man wearing a wide-brimmed hat and a tool belt was bent over by the edge of the shrubs adjusting something hidden in the grass. When I got closer, I saw it was the head of a sprinkler. He had his back to me and didn't see or hear me coming.

"Hola," I said, hoping I didn't scare him, but he seemed unfazed. He had blond hair and a ruddy, weather-beaten complexion. He smiled at me. "Hey there," he said in what sounded like a Southern drawl.

"Are you from the U.S.?" I asked.

"Yep. Atlanta."

"Me too. I mean, about the U.S. I'm from New Jersey."

"I'm Rick," he said, extending his hand.

"Piper."

"What brings you down here?" he asked.

"I'm studying Spanish with a language group. We live on the other side of campus."

He nodded and wiped his brow with a red handkerchief. "Oh right. I heard a few Americans were studying here. Enjoying yourself?"

"It's cool," I replied. "What about you?"

"I'm with the hotel group. We're still prepping the property for the reno. You'll be seeing us around, I'm sure."

"What hotel group?" I asked.

"Capwell Resorts. They bought this place to turn it into a hotel and marina." He motioned toward the buildings around him. "We'll be razing these in the next few weeks. Hopefully, the construction noise won't be too much."

"This place is going to be a hotel? What about the school?"

"I don't know what the island is doing about a

school, but this property is for sure going to be a resort."

"But the dorms?" I motioned to the buildings where Julian lived.

"Those things? Condemned. Already gutted inside. Nothing but spiders and ants."

"Y-you mean no one lives here?"

"No, not a soul. Your buildings are the only ones intact. Why? Is something wrong?"

"No, no," I murmured. "I just didn't know they were moving the school."

He looked confused. "There hasn't been a school here for a while. It was closed down. Gosh, I think about two years ago now."

The look of desertion. The disorganized library. I should have known. I barely managed to say goodbye as I backed away. No wonder the grounds were desolate. And Julian. He had lied outright to me. He wasn't living in the dorm. He wasn't even a student here.

No one was.

I thought back to the day I met him. How he had appeared suddenly in the library and pretended to have been innocently looking for a book when I jumped out at him. The library incident had happened the very day after I met the general. *Had his father put him up to it?* I felt sick. When I find Julian, I thought, I am going to kill him. I am going murder the guy with my bare hands. And to think I had trusted him. Liked him even.

At the pool, I dropped into my favorite lounge chair. The sun was still out and shining brightly, and I was grateful because the latest shock had chilled me. Thankfully Coco wasn't there yet so I could pull myself together, but I wished I could just go back to my room. All the anxiety was making me brutally tired. I leaned back in the lounge chair and tried to breathe deeply to calm my rising panic.

I contemplated what I was going to say to Julian when, or if, I saw him again. I wondered if I should I confront him outright and demand an answer. Or if I should play up to him and try to get him to fess up about whatever charade he was involved with. There were so many strategies to consider, I was even starting to get a little excited. I would show that loser precisely who he was messing with. He thought my little scene at the restaurant was a bad one. Well, that was nothing compared to how I would embarrass him next.

I was somewhere between a state of sleeping and semi-consciousness when I heard, or should I say smelled, Coco walk up to me. She had clearly doused herself in expensive perfume. My lids were so heavy under my sunglasses, I could barely open them to greet her, and for a few seconds, I prayed she would let me sleep in peace.

The lounge chair next to me creaked as she sat down and stretched out. I turned my head a little to the side and peered through my half-closed eyes. Her arm was draped over the edge of the chair, and for the first time, I noticed how beautiful her hands were. Her tanned fingers were thin and long, and her French manicure was interesting. Instead of having the tips of her nails painted white, they were dark purple. And on the underside of her wrist was a tattoo of a large black cross. I wondered when she had taken the time to plaster on a fake tattoo.

"Okay, Coco," I said as I sat up and pulled my sunglasses off. "I'm ready."

But Coco was nowhere in sight.

Next to me in the lounge chair, sitting almost so close she could reach out and touch me, was a Black Mariah.

17

The Black Mariah

I sprung out of my chair so fast the contents of my purse scattered all over the cement pool deck. One of my lipsticks rolled toward the edge of the pool and came within inches of plopping in. I had no idea if I should start picking things up, holler for help, or simply say hello as though a nun sat down within inches of my beach chair every day. Since I didn't know what to do, I did the only thing I could think of —nothing.

"I'm sorry to have startled you," she said coolly.

Her accent, like Julian's, was hard to place. Both of them sounded as if they were trying to fake a British accent but weren't quite getting it right.

She was wearing the Mariahs' long black silk gown

with a high veil on her head. Only this nun's veil covered her face so I couldn't quite make out her features. Though, even with the veil, I could see she was wearing fake eyelashes and more makeup than a Las Vegas showgirl. She was smiling as though we were old friends.

"I was expecting someone else," I said. I looked in the direction of the dorm. *Where the heck was Coco when I needed her?* I bent down to pick up my pens, my wallet, my cell phone, and my makeup. The nun watched me, fascinated, as though she had never seen a purse before.

"I...can I, ah, help you with something?" I asked.

"You look like the one who needs help," she replied. She rose gracefully from the chair and picked up the lipstick teetering on the pool's edge. I took it from her and stuffed it into my purse.

"Excuse me?" I replied.

"You are in danger, you know. I am a friend."

"Danger?"

"Yes, darling." She sat back down in the lounge chair.

"What danger are you talking about?"

"Associations."

"Associations? Meaning?"

"I'm talking about associations of the worst sort. You know who I am referring to. No need to pretend you do not."

"Julian Castillo?" I asked.

"Of course."

I waited for an explanation, but she remained silent.

I thought back to Julian and his pack of lies. "You're a day late and a dollar short with that warning," I said.

"I'm afraid I don't understand."

"Never mind. I was just being sarcastic."

"Then you know already?"

We couldn't possibly be talking about the same thing. "I know what already?" I asked.

She raised an eyebrow. "You don't know then?"

"How am I to know whether or not I know, if you don't tell me what it is you think I don't know?"

She opened her mouth to say something but closed it again.

"Maybe you ought to just tell me what's going on," I said. "Especially considering you went through all the trouble of sneaking up on me."

She gave me a broad smile. "Similar to the way you crept up to our northern gate."

"It was a minor instance of trespassing. Please, would you tell me what is going on?"

"Malfaedra will explain. She wants to see you. She sent me to invite you to dinner. I am the only one who knows my way around this place. I used to be a student here, you know, before this." She gestured at her regalia.

As she did, I glimpsed Coco exiting the lobby door and heading toward us. When the nun saw Coco, she stood up. "How unfortunate. I was hoping we would have more time before your fashion discussion. Can you come tomorrow?"

"To the convent?"

"Yes. You already know the way."

Tea with the murderous island dictator, dinner with the head of the local cult. I was sure getting popular. "I'll think about it," I replied.

"Good. I will tell Malfaedra to expect you when your classes end."

"I said I'll think about it."

She leaned over and placed her hand on my arm. "Believe me, we are not the ones you have to fear. But you should take warning, and I suggest you do not delay in learning about your situation."

"That's a little ominous, but okay."

"I don't mean to scare you." She lowered her voice. "But I would recommend you stay in your room tonight and lock the doors. Or stay with your friend. If I was followed, we have some concern."

"Oh, that makes it much less ominous, thank you."

She smiled at me before leaving in a flourish, a rush of perfume following in her wake.

"Were you talking to one of those nuns?" Coco asked when she finally reached the pool.

"Yes."

"What did she want?"

"Um, directions."

"Directions? Doesn't she live here?"

"She wanted to get into the library, but I told her it was closed."

"Can't even," she said.

"What?"

"I can't even deal with that right now."

"Me neither, believe me."

Coco sat down in the lounge chair the nun had vacated and pulled out her laptop. It had a silver glitter cover. "Should we get started?" she asked.

"Let me see where you left off."

She opened a document she had saved to her desktop with my name on it. All she had written was the title: "Why Fashion is Art."

"Well, I guess that's a start," I said. I took my journal and a pen out of my purse. Maybe if she told me exactly what it was that made her enthusiastic about the industry, it would be a good enough argument to interest her judges.

"Okay, Coco, I have an idea."

"You do? Great!"

"I'll ask you questions, and you answer them with the first thought that comes to mind. You know, not with what you think they want to hear. I'm sure we can get to the root of a really great essay." I wasn't sure, but I didn't know what else to do.

"Perfect," she said. "Ask away."

I turned to a blank page and then paused. How had the nun known what I was meeting Coco about? I looked down toward the empty stretch of beach, but she was gone.

"What now?" Coco asked.

"Nothing, nothing," I said. "I was just thinking."

"Aren't you going to ask me a question?"

"Right," I said. "Yes."

But my mind was going in a thousand different directions and none of them involved Coco's essay.

18

The Observer in the Mangroves

After an hour of attempting to make sense of exactly what Coco wanted to do in the fashion world, my thoughts started drifting back to Julian. And to my visit from the Black Mariah. I contemplated what I was going to do if Julian showed up at my door later, and I figured he would. After all, he didn't know I had found out he lied to me about living at the school. And it wasn't like he was still mad at me for my madcap exit from the restaurant. He was the one who said we were dating, not me.

"Did you hear what I just said?" Coco asked.

"No."

"I said let's take a break and get dinner before all the good stuff is gone."

"All right, but Coco, we should really finish this. Why don't we eat quickly and then go back to your room and get it done?"

"Okay, but fair warning, my artistic sensibilities mean I see the world better through chaos."

"Huh?"

"My room is a mess."

"Mine is too. Who cares?" I stood up and slung my purse over my shoulder. "How is it you can say a sentence like that but write an essay so badly?"

Coco looked crestfallen. "Is it really that hopeless?" she asked.

"Coco, I'm kidding. You didn't write anything except for the title."

"I edited the whole thing."

I burst out laughing. "You sure did."

She squeezed my arm. "I knew you would be able to help. You are so artsy."

"Artsy?" I replied. "I don't think so."

"No, you totally are. Like artsy in the way you are confident about being different."

"Thanks a lot."

"No, Piper, I mean it in a nice way!"

"Okay, Coco, whatever. Let's go."

The dinner buffet was already set up in steaming silver platters. Coco grabbed a plate from the far end of the table. "I wonder what's on the menu tonight," she said. She lifted a lid off the catering tray and sighed.

"Oh, the same old chicken skewers." She put about ten skewers on her plate and about three more on mine.

I followed her out the glass doors to the round tables by the lobby pool where everyone else was sitting. We sat down with Aisling and Gareth, but as they all started talking about going downtown after dinner, my mind wandered off again.

The whole Julian thing still had me puzzled. Why would he have lied to me about living on campus knowing any second I could find out the university had been closed down for good? And furthermore, if he didn't live on campus why was he hanging around an out-of-business library on a random Sunday? All I could come up with was that his father put him up to it as a way to meet me. But why? Just because I looked like their priestess? That seemed a little extreme. Regard-less, as angry as I was, I couldn't help but occasionally glance toward the front door of the lobby to see if his car was pulling up.

"What do you think, Piper?" Gareth asked.

"Sorry," I said, looking up. "I missed it. What were you talking about?"

"Girl, you are in space," Aisling said.

"Must be the new guy," Coco said. "Is that why you keep looking over there?" She dropped her fork on the glass table and it made a loud clanking noise. "But you can't go out with him tonight. You promised to help me."

"I'm going to help you. I'm definitely not seeing him tonight. But I missed what you were all saying."

"I asked what you think about the storm," Gareth said.

"What storm? I don't know anything about a storm."

"It's all over the news," he replied.

"What news are you watching?" I asked. "I don't even have a television."

"Gareth is being impossible," Aisling said. "We heard about it on television at this little café downtown. Apparently, a hurricane is coming, but the entire forecast was in Spanish so maybe we missed something."

"My dad told me it was hurricane season," I said.

"Did he tell you about Lila?" Gareth asked.

"Who?"

"Hurricane Lila," Gareth said, mimicking a weatherman's deep voice. "They just named the storm. It's a few hundred miles off Grenada right now, but is heading right for us."

"Perfect," I said. "As long as it doesn't stop us from going home on time, I don't care if it hits."

"You don't like it here much, do you, Piper?" Aisling asked.

"It's not that," I said. How was I going to explain what the real problem was? That I was being chased like a mouse by a bunch of nuns, a ruthless general, and now even possibly his son? "I'm just a little homesick. Tomorrow is the Fourth of July."

"You don't exactly strike me as the lawn party type," Aisling said.

"Thanks a lot."

"Don't make her mad, Aisling," Coco wailed. "She is a major patriot."

I smiled at Coco.

"I, for one, hope the storm hits," Aisling said. "I've never been in a hurricane before. It sounds exciting. What's the worst that could happen?"

"We could lose power for days and you won't be able to straighten your hair with your hair dryer," I said.

"My hair is naturally straight," Aisling replied, stroking her stick-straight hair that had a suspicious curl right at the top of her part.

Coco snorted. "If Lila hits, we'll find out if that's true."

"Like you are one to talk, your hair drips with keratin," Aisling said.

"It's a conditioning treatment! Are you ready, Piper? I'm done, and I don't want dessert, do you?"

I shook my head and looked down at my half-eaten plate. I couldn't have finished it if I tried. My stomach was still a knot of nerves.

We dropped off our plates in the bin set up for dirty dishes, and I trailed behind Coco as we walked through the front door. I wanted to brush off the Black Mariah's warning about me being in danger, but considering everything else that had happened, I wasn't so sure I should.

Darkness had finally set in, and for the first time since I had arrived, I noticed the stars were gone and the moon was missing too. The sky was coal black, as though someone had draped a cloth over the entire island. Despite Coco's happy chattering, I still felt uneasy as we climbed the steps to our rooms.

Something else was out of order, but it took me a moment to figure out what it was. Then I realized it was the overhead lights. The ones illuminating the stairwell and the exterior hallways of our building were extinguished.

"What's the matter?" Coco asked.

"The lights," I murmured.

"What about them?"

"They're off."

Coco shrugged. "So what?"

I didn't respond because I caught a whiff of something putrid in the air. I recognized the scent almost instantly. It was from a cigar. It was thick and permeating like the ones my dad and his cronies smoked on occasion after dinner at the Officers' Club.

"Do you smell that?" I asked.

Coco sniffed around like a dog. "Not really, but I'm all stuffy."

I leaned over the railing, but I couldn't see anything

except the faint outline of the mangrove tree line. The smell was strong, and it was definitely coming from somewhere beneath us. I took a few cautious steps forward, and then I heard the crunching of mulch and twigs from someone else's footsteps. I paused and listened. The crunching stopped too. I tilted my head and moved forward again. The mulch crackled. Someone was following us. I was sure of it.

I squinted into the night, keeping my eyes trained on the tree line. There was the tiniest hint of red flame flickering against the foliage. Someone was definitely hiding in the bushes smoking a cigar. I could see the red tip glow hot and then dissipate, glow hot and then dissipate.

"What are you doing?" Coco asked.

"Be quiet," I whispered and put my finger on my lips.

"Why?"

"Just hush, just for a second."

As I continued to watch the trees, the glowing red tip of the cigar began to move through the shrubbery toward us.

"What's going on, Piper?" Coco whispered.

"Shhh," I replied.

I knew we should probably run, but I couldn't take my eyes away from the glowing cigar. Maybe it was just one of the general's watchers, but why was he hiding in the shrubs and not on patrol like a normal security guard? And the Black Mariah's warning was not helping matters.

The bushes rustled and I saw a dark figure make his way rapidly toward the stairwell. Without any light, I couldn't make out a face. All I could tell was that the man was very large. I watched as he put his hand into his pocket. Next to me, I could hear Coco say something about how I was scaring her, but I could only pay attention to what was about to come out of the man's pocket. There was a flash of something shiny and a quickening of footsteps.

"Knife!" I cried. "Run!"

"Knife?" Coco repeated.

I grabbed her arm. "Come on, we've got to go!"

She tripped as I nearly dragged her down the hall to her door. "You're scaring me, Piper," she whined, but I didn't slow down. If she was scared, I was terrified. "Hurry up," I told her. "Where is your key?"

"Oh, it's, um..." Coco began fumbling with her purse. She pulled her key out, but her hand was shaking too much to unlock the door. I yanked the key away from her and with a steadiness I didn't know I possessed, I slid the key into the lock and turned it. I shoved Coco into her room and slammed the door behind us.

"What happened?" Coco asked. She put her hands on her hips and waited for an explanation.

I was faced with two options. Either tell Coco

everything and hope she didn't spill it to the entire group or make up a story.

"Robbers," I whispered.

"What robbers?"

"There are robbers in the mangroves. No one told you?"

"No! I've walked past the mangroves a thousand times."

"They only come out at night." I felt terrible lying, especially if the guy was just one of the general's stupid watchers out there smoking a cigar.

"I've been at the pool at night."

"Well, these are robbers who only like to pick on pairs of people. They get more money that way. Two women, two purses. No sense robbing only one, and any more than two is hard." It sounded like the dumbest explanation on the planet, but I had no choice.

Coco looked skeptical, but she gave me a big hug. "Gosh Piper, I think you totally saved my life tonight."

"I don't actually know if it was a robber," I said, disentangling myself from her embrace. "I was only guessing. Better to be safe than sorry. Listen, why don't we forget all about it and work on the essay?"

Coco nodded, still smiling at me like I was her knight in shining armor. She turned on all the lights in her room. Clothes were strewn everywhere, and on top of them were bikinis and mismatched shoes. "Sorry for the mess," she said.

"That's okay, you should see my room." The thought caused a pain in my chest. It was a long, dark walk away.

"Coco, the, um, robber really spooked me. Can I crash with you tonight?" I asked. "We can work on your essay as late as you want, maybe even finish it." If Julian stopped by, he would have to knock on every door if he wanted to find me.

Coco sat down on her bed. "Really, finish it? Okay, great. I totally know what you mean about the robber. He might decide to attack a lone person after all."

"Yes, exactly."

Coco started scrambling around under her bed and tried to dislodge one of her leopard print suitcases. "You are not going to believe what I brought with me from home in case of an emergency. I've been waiting for the right time to open it."

"Can't wait." I took a deep breath and sat down in her chair. It was probably a stack of fashion magazines I would be forced to pore over. Fashion magazines or death by cigar man? It was a tough decision, but if I wanted to stay in her room, I had to keep her happy.

Coco gave one final tug, and her suitcase came loose. She unzipped it and I plastered a fake smile on my face. But when I saw what she pulled out, I laughed. It was an entire package of peanut butter cookies.

She held them up triumphantly. "I haven't opened them yet. I was afraid I would eat them all at once."

Coco peeled the plastic back from the top of the package before offering it to me.

I took a bite and smiled. It tasted like home. "Coco, I think you're great," I said. And I meant it. For the first time in my life, I was really happy to have a girlfriend.

19

Return to the Convent

When I woke up the next morning on the edge of Coco's bed, my first thought was how Julian had lied to me. And I was furious. I thought of all the clever things I could do and say to manipulate him the way he was apparently trying to manipulate me.

Maybe I was taking things a bit far but plotting against him was making me feel better. A voice in my head kept saying, "He was cute and smart and a gentleman, and I thought he really liked me for who I am." Stupid girl, I cursed. Julian may have acted like a gentleman, but I was going to be the smarter one. And I could only be smarter if I put aside my childish feelings and started thinking about my next move.

Coco was still fast asleep with a gold satin face mask covering her eyes. It was only six thirty so I could have slept for another hour, but I wanted to get back to my room and change since I had slept in my clothes. I'd declined her offer of lending me something from her assortment of lace nightgowns and silk lingerie.

I sat up quietly and pulled my dreadlocks back into a ponytail with the hair elastic I always keep around my wrist. I tiptoed to the door, but as my hand touched the knob, I remembered the smell of the cigar. Had someone really been down there stalking me with a knife or had my mind been playing tricks on me? And maybe it was just a maintenance man or one of the new contractors. But why had the lights been out? I shivered despite myself.

The latch clicked loudly as I opened the door. Coco didn't stir, so I stepped outside and closed the door behind me. The sun was low in the sky, and for a moment, I paused and inhaled the tropical air. The sweet smell I noticed the first day I arrived was still there, but there was another smell too—the ocean. For a second, it reminded me so much of New Jersey, I felt at peace. And then I remembered the date and a wave of homesickness washed over me. It was the Fourth of July.

The hallway was empty in both directions, so I hurried to my room. The uneasy feeling I had didn't disappear until my own door was locked securely behind me. I took a quick look around, but nothing was out of place. Immediately, I checked by the door for a note from Julian, but no matter how many times I looked, there was nothing. I clenched my teeth. The least he could do after going through all the trouble of tricking me into liking him would be to continue to pursue me.

After I showered and dressed, I double-checked the locks on my balcony door and front door before I headed to the lobby. The parking lot was empty, and the palm trees and mangrove bushes lining the edge of the property looked undisturbed. Off in the distance, I could see Pilar setting up our breakfast in the lobby. Something about her presence as she bustled around made me feel better.

I tried to figure out where Coco and I had been standing when I first smelled the cigar. The shrubbery surrounding the building was so dense anyone could hide in it if they wanted to. Cautiously, I stepped into the mulch and ducked below a colossal hibiscus plant. From where I stood, I had a direct sightline to the lobby pool. I imagined a man watching us, noting when we stood up and cleaned off our plates. I turned around and looked behind me. There was a clean-cut path leading away from the lobby to the octagon dormitories. It would have been easy for him to keep an eye on us as we made our way across the parking lot.

I crouched down and searched the ground for ashes,

but it had rained during the night. If there had been ashes, they had long since been absorbed. Then, just as I stepped out of the bush, I heard a crunch under my foot. A long, thin plastic cigar wrapper was partially hidden in the mulch. The guy could have at least had the decency to throw it in a wastebasket, I thought. Despite my nerves, I had to laugh a little. Here someone was potentially tracking me—or maybe even definitely tracking me if I were to believe the Black Mariah's ominous warning—and I was worried about whether or not he was recycling.

I picked up the wrapper and made my way to the lobby, praying the pay phone was working because I wanted to call home again. Then I remembered the last incident with the operator who had never asked Becky to accept the charges. Did I risk someone listening in on my conversation? I thought about it for a second then pushed my worries aside. All I wanted to do was wish my dad and Becky a happy Fourth of July. Two days ago, I had been prepared to tell him to buy me a plane ticket off the island, but now there was no way in hell I was leaving. I needed to settle the score with Julian.

I picked up the receiver, pressed zero, and waited. At first, nothing happened. I tried again and heard the loud click and the sound of the female operator yelling in my ear. She asked all the same questions she had the first time I got through. When my dad answered the phone, she even barked her command about accepting the charges.

"Hey kiddo," my dad said when he heard my voice. "That was your promptest response yet. I see you got my message."

"What message?"

"You didn't get it?"

"No," I replied. "I didn't get a message."

"I sent you a fax yesterday. I had to walk all over the base, and I finally located the Air Force's last working fax machine in one of the offices. I had no other way to reach you. I called the main number at the Institute, and they said the best way to ensure a message goes through is to send a fax."

"I never got it. What's wrong?"

"Have you been watching the news?"

"Um, Dad, there is not much news down here. What happened?"

"Big storm out there, kid, moving north to north-west at ten miles per hour."

"I did hear something about that. Two of my friends caught the weather at a café downtown."

"Well, what's the Institute planning to do about it? The lady at the main number is sitting in some office in New York City, and she didn't get what I was saying."

"What exactly are you saying, Dad?"

"Your ass is going to get hit by a hurricane is what I am saying!"

I sighed. Despite what Gareth had told us the night before, my father was a bit of an alarmist where the weather was concerned. I always figured it was because he was flying to far-flung destinations, usually after a natural disaster hit the place.

"How high above sea level is this school of yours?"

I looked through the glass windows of the lobby at the dark-blue sea that was flat as glass. Even with the seawall, I wasn't naive enough to believe if a major hurricane landed, we wouldn't have a big problem on our hands.

"How high above sea level? Um, maybe six..."

"Sixty? Sixty feet?"

"Ah, no, six feet in some places at worst, I would say."

"Six feet! Christ!" he exclaimed. "Then they need an evacuation plan, and they need one now."

"I'm sure they have one, Dad."

"Then what is it?"

"They will probably tell us today. In fact, I'm sure of it. Now that the storm is confirmed, they are bound to have some idea of how we're going to stay safe."

His deep Air Force voice came out. "They had better be doing something. And they had better let me know exactly what it is."

"Yes, Dad, they will. I'm sure I will hear today."

"I want you to call me as soon as you know the plan, do you understand?"

I was tempted to yell, "Yes, sir!" but I settled for, "Sure, of course. I will be in touch as soon as I know what they are going to do."

The line filled with static and then there was a loud snap. "Can you hear me?" I asked. "Dad? Dad?" But there was only the silence of dead air. "Happy Fourth of July," I whispered.

It took me a moment to compose myself because I wanted nothing more than to somehow beam myself home, crawl into my narrow bed in my little room, and pull my red comforter right over my head.

The rest of the day was a blur. I spent most of it staring listlessly out the window of the Reef Room when it wasn't my turn to play Cecilia's latest intercultural understanding game. Contrary to what I told my father, the hurricane was only touched on briefly.

"The Institute is in touch with headquarters, we are monitoring the storm, and additional information will be forthcoming," Cecilia said with an unconcerned smile.

Gareth began talking about storm paths, but Cecilia shook her head and explained the Institute had dealt with everything from government instability to earthquakes to hurricanes, so we had nothing to worry about. "I have every confidence we will be well-prepared and informed if the hurricane poses a threat to our safety."

Satisfied we were taken care of, I let my mind drift to Julian and my looming visit to the convent. I thought about the randomness of the timing. Had I not run into the landscaper moments before the Black Mariah approached me, I would never have known Julian had been lying to me the entire time we were together. I would never have believed the nun when she said I was in danger because of my "associations."

When class finally let out for the day, I tried to make a quick exit, but Coco called my name and chased me into the hall. We'd had a good time the night before, but I had assumed once I finished her essay, she would simply leave me alone.

"Hey," she said when I stopped and turned around. "Where are you running off to? Don't you want to have dinner?"

"No, thanks. I'm going for a walk, actually. I need to find Julian," I added quickly before she offered to come with me.

"Aren't you forgetting something?" she asked.

I paused for a second, but I didn't know what she was talking about. "What am I forgetting?" I asked.

"I owe you this." She reached into her little pink clutch and pulled out a crumpled wad of hundred-dollar bills. "There should be five hundred there," she said. She held it out, but I didn't take the money.

"Here," she said, shaking her hand at me. "What are you waiting for? It's yours like I promised."

"Coco," I started, feeling guilty all of a sudden. It was too much money—way too much for the little work

I had done, even if she had driven me crazy for days. I shook my head. "It's way too much. I can't take money from you."

"But that was our agreement," she protested. "You really helped me. I reread the essay while we were sitting in class today, and it is so much better than what I could have written. I want you to have it."

I looked at the crumpled-up bills again. It was tempting, but I couldn't bring myself to take it. "Keep it, Coco. It wasn't a big deal, really."

She sighed and pouted. "Are you sure?"

I nodded.

"Then let me treat you to dinner or something downtown one night," she said.

"Okay, fair enough."

Before I could stop her, she leaped forward and hugged me. "Thank you, Piper! You are the bestest friend ever!"

I couldn't help but laugh as I hugged her back.

"Have fun with your boyfriend," she said.

"Um, thanks, I will," I said. If she only knew where I was really going.

I walked slowly in the direction of the salt water pool and headed for the path to the beach. I had to admit I was kind of spooked about going to the convent by myself. And what if the cigar man was waiting for me in the bushes or down by the stream where the foliage was thick?

I took a deep breath. If I could get down to the beach unharmed and unseen, then I would be able to follow the same route I took the last time and cling to the bushes lining the shore. I looked over my shoulder once and then darted down the path and across the stream. I didn't stop running until I reached the empty stretch of beach. I pushed myself up into the mangroves as far as I could and looked in both directions. Once again, the beach was desolate and quiet. Even the ocean was almost still. It was difficult to believe there was a storm brewing out there somewhere.

I tried to keep my nerves under control as the convent wall covered in sea heather came into sight. I climbed the spiral staircase and pushed the sea heather to the side where I remembered the gate was hidden and then paused. I wondered if I should turn the knob and walk right in or knock loudly on the door first. I didn't have to think about it for long because as I reached my hand up in a fist to knock, the gate swung open and the Black Mariah who had approached me at the pool stood there smiling.

✺ 2 0 ✺

The Gift of the Past

She knew she'd startled me again and she smirked, obviously entertained by my fright. She was dressed in her full habit, only this time her veil was not covering her face. I was staring at her perfect features and wondering if they made plastic surgery part of their vows when it dawned on me who she was.

The mystery housekeeper.

Then she could have also been the one in my room. She must have hung the rosary. And makeup freak that she was, she'd probably also tried on my old pharmacy eyeliner, which explained why my toiletry bag had been moved.

"Hello, Piper," she said. "You are right on time."

"I wasn't aware we had set a time."

"Malfaedra is very much looking forward to your visit. By the way, I don't think I ever properly introduced myself. My name is Orchid. Like the flower." She extended her hand. It was cool and smooth and reminded me of a cold stone.

"We have met three times now, haven't we?" I asked. "Only the first time, you were running around pretending to be a housekeeper."

"Yes," she replied. "Of course."

"It was you who broke into my room too then, wasn't it?"

"Of course."

"Why? What did you want, other than to scare me half to death? And was the housekeeper outfit really necessary? I want answers."

Orchid smiled, but she didn't respond.

"Forget it," I continued. "I already know why you did it. Work at the convent is too slow for you, so you sneak out at night to join the fast-paced world of custodians. Secretly under your gown, you are wearing a lace apron and carrying a bottle of cleaning spray."

"I don't know what you mean, Piper. I'm having a hard time following your American sarcasm."

Her serene composure irritated me. "What I'm asking is why were you dressed as a housekeeper? And why did you break into my room?"

"I couldn't very well go in dressed like this." She gestured to her gown.

"If you are not going to explain, then I'm out of here. Good luck explaining to your boss, or whatever she is, how you managed to ruin her dinner plans."

"Piper," she said in a singsong voice, "there is no need for hysterics."

"I'm not hysterical, I'm frustrated."

"There is no need for frustration, either."

"Then answer the question. Why were you in my room?"

"To investigate, of course."

"Investigate? What is there to investigate?"

"Many things."

"Explain please."

"It is not for me to say," Orchid replied.

"Then who will?"

"Malfaedra was the one who sent me to your room, and she is the one who will explain all there is to explain. Now will you please let me escort you inside? It is all I have been trying to do right along."

"No, I have one more question."

"All right."

"Why did you hang up the rosary? Was it some scare tactic of yours? Did you want me to have a sleepless night?"

"Is that what happened?" she asked.

"Yes!"

She let out a little peal of laughter. "I hung it over your bed for protection, Piper. Our rosaries are either on our person at all times or else hanging over our beds. It is the custom of our order and it keeps us safe from harm. To do anything else is sacrilegious and sure to bring evil to our door."

"So, you hung the thing up for my own protection?"

"Of course."

"And you didn't think I would see it hanging there and panic because someone had been in my room?"

"I assumed you knew the custom and what was proper, but perhaps forgot."

"How the hell would I know the custom?"

"You possess the rosary, do you not?"

"For your information, someone gave it to me."

Orchid frowned. "And this person did not explain its power?"

"No, she pressed it into my hand, mumbled something, and split."

"Who gave you this treasured gift? You must tell me. Only our true followers own them, and they are not likely to be given away."

I thought of Clara and her abrupt handoff of the rosary. If she had one, then she must be loyal to the Black Mariahs, but then why would she be working in the general's house? Maybe she was a nun dressed as a housekeeper too. Regardless, I still felt bad betraying her to anyone.

"Fine, I found it. In Carabajel. It must have fallen off someone's neck."

She narrowed her eyes and I assume she guessed I was lying, but she quickly gave me an overly patient smile. "You must remember, Piper, we are your only true friends here."

"Is that right? And being my true friend means breaking into my room to investigate, moving a rosary, and stealing a note from Julian Castillo?"

Orchid wrinkled her pert little nose at the mention of his name. "I told you already. You are in grave danger in his company. We were only trying to prevent you from associating with him."

"Sure, whatever."

"It is futile for us to bicker like this when Malfaedra is waiting for you. She will help you understand everything. She will leave you without any doubt or fear." She reached for my arm. "Come, let us walk together as the sisters we are."

I shook my head in exasperation, stepped through the gate, and instinctively recoiled. Directly behind Orchid was a steep chasm that dropped straight into the sea. The entire time she had been talking to me, she'd been balanced precariously right on the edge. It was such an optical illusion. When I saw the nun swimming that day, I had no idea I was standing on the edge of an abyss.

"God, is this some kind of mantrap?" I asked,

looking down. I was also sort of glad she was still holding my arm, but I wasn't about to admit it.

"We never know who is going to try to open the gate."

"Maybe a lock would come in handy."

She giggled. "Yes, but it is so much more fun to rescue intruders from the ocean. Most of us are expert swimmers. There is the rail." She pointed into the sea heather where an old wood banister was partially hidden in the brush. "The stairs are up ahead."

I followed her lead across the ledge, walking hesitantly and trying not to look down. I marveled at how she trotted along without ever once having to hold on to steady herself.

When we reached the circular staircase leading down to the beach, Orchid lifted her hem up just enough to reveal black, stiletto heels with silk ribbons that wrapped around her ankles. They looked like cruel punishment by shoes, but I couldn't help but think Coco would probably love them.

I paused on the top step, my nerves getting the better of me.

"What's wrong?" Orchid asked, turning around. She shaded her eyes from the setting sun and blinked. She must have been wearing at least two pairs of fake eyelashes.

"Nothing," I lied. Meeting Malfaedra in a convent was enough to bring on an anxiety attack. I certainly hadn't needed a tightrope walk on the edge of a cliff. I took a step down onto the metal staircase and followed her until my feet hit the sand.

The convent loomed above us and was even more imposing than the first time I had glimpsed it.

"It is beautiful, isn't it?" Orchid asked with a tone of reverence.

"Yes," I said. "Actually, this island is the most beautiful place I have ever seen, even if I don't know what's going on."

"You really don't know?"

"No, I really don't. All I know is I resemble one of your saints, that Vella person."

She nodded and said something in a low voice, but I didn't hear her.

"What did you say?" I asked.

"Can I ask you a question?"

"Go for it."

"I was wondering," she said, "do you know Mary Kay?"

It took a second for the question to register, and when it did, I stood there dumbstruck. The lady with the pink car? Was she joking?

"Um, what?" I asked.

"You know, Mary Kay, the makeup lady."

"No! I know who she is, but I don't use her make-up."

Mary Kay was a big deal in Dallas. I remembered

driving downtown with my dad once when her company was having an event at the convention center. The street had been jam-packed with pink cars. I told her about my recollection, though I had no idea whether she knew where Dallas was or even what a convention center was.

"Oh, you're lucky," she purred. "It must have been so glamorous."

We were way off topic. I mean, of all the silly things to bring up. Mary Kay? What was next? "Look, I don't really wear makeup," I said.

Orchid looked disappointed by my reaction. Her smile quickly turned into a pouty frown.

"Is that what you were looking for in my makeup bag?" I asked, folding my arms across my chest. "Mary Kay's make-up?"

"I thought maybe you had some. I've always wanted to try it. I thought everyone in the States wore it."

"I can't believe we are really talking about makeup. No, not everyone wears it. In some areas maybe they do, but no one I know. How do you know about it?"

"I found a catalogue once at the school. But they don't deliver down here."

I covered my eyes with my hands. "Can't even," I said.

"Can't even what?" she asked innocently.

"I can't even believe I am having this conversation. In America, I don't think nuns wear makeup."

"Good thing we are not in America then."

I was past the point of trying to make sense out of the conversation. "Right, of course," I replied. "Good thing."

Orchid started to walk up the hill past their swimming pool toward the back of the convent. She glanced over her shoulder to make sure I was following her. I was starting to feel a little bit like a lost dog.

"I'd like to get back to the saint I resemble. Vella," I said, and Orchid stopped walking. She didn't look happy.

"Yes. Santa Vella. Are you trying to trick me?"

"Me, trick you? Try the other way around."

"Malfaedra will see I was right all along."

"I am not following you," I said.

"Yes, you are."

"I mean I am not keeping up with your logic."

"I told Malfaedra that it is quite possible you don't know anything, and your being here is just a coincidence."

Not again with the coincidence, I thought. I was about to say as much when she continued speaking.

"You see, Malfaedra said it was impossible that you don't know. She asked why you would be on Carabajel, of all places, if you don't know?"

"Don't know what?" I asked, but she ignored the question.

"I reminded her that not all of us believe it when it

happens, or even pay any attention to it. I did not truly believe it until I was fully indoctrinated into the Order of the Black Mariahs. Then I learned how to rein it in."

I felt my chest heave with annoyance. Why did everyone on the island have a flipping gift for never getting to the point? "Rein what in?" I asked. "I am still not following your logic."

"Rein in the gift we have. The gift of reincarnation." She stepped closer to me and put her hands on my shoulders. "You see, my sister," she said, "there are those of us here who can see the past."

Malfaedra

I struggled to make sense of her words. *There are those of us here who can see the past.*

I wanted to tell her I didn't know what she was talking about. The problem was, I had a horrifying feeling I did know. The déjà vu. The fountain at the airport. The pier with the torch. The staircase hidden alongside the ruins. The cemetery under the rotary.

Orchid was watching me intensely. When I didn't say anything, her expression turned smug.

"So, you do know," she said.

"Yes," I confessed. "Maybe. I—I'm not sure. There are places here that are familiar, but I've never been here before. I've never even left the States before this trip."

"Yes, my sister," she said. "You have indeed."

"No, I really haven't."

"Not in this lifetime perhaps. You must understand the past we can see is our own. The lives we have lived before this one."

I turned around and looked at the pier behind me. Was it possible? All of the visions I'd had and the dreams. I thought of my mother again. Had she had the same affliction? The same gift? A gift that was an affliction?

"We better go," Orchid said, linking her arm with mine. "Malfaedra does not like to be kept waiting. Don't worry, we were all daunted when we realized we had the gift. It is natural to be taken aback."

"Yeah, because it's not natural to have this so-called gift."

"It is the same as any mystery, is it not? Come along, Piper. It is Malfaedra you should be speaking to. There are rules here and I fear I have said too much already."

I gazed up at the convent and thought of the time when I was about nine years old and my dad and I drove from Texas to New Orleans to visit my grandma. I loved going there because her tiny kitchen was always stockpiled with pralines. She also listened to everything I said with rapt attention.

In those days, I was obsessed with Amelia Earhart and wanted nothing more than to be an aviatrix like her. In retrospect, I probably should have chosen a better pilot considering she crashed her plane. But my father had bought me a leather flying cap, and I wore it everywhere with my swim goggles. When I showed up in my outfit at my grandma's house, she exclaimed, "My goodness, you are Amelia Earhart reincarnated!"

I'd rolled the word "reincarnated" around on my tongue for a minute before asking her what it meant.

"Being reincarnated means you lived a past life as someone else." My grandma started to launch into a whole explanation until my dad finally interrupted her with some remark about science and hogwash. But it was too late. The damage was done, and I'd spent the entire next year insisting I was Amelia Earhart back from the dead.

"Wait," I said, thinking of something and shaking my arm free again from Orchid's grasp. "Orchid, you all don't actually believe I am the second coming of your Santa Vella person, do you? Because I look like her?"

It would explain everything. The Black Mariahs' interest in me. The unprecedented attention from the general. The awed looks I got from the locals. The general's chauffeur fleeing from the bakery at the sight of me.

"Of course," Orchid replied.

"But that's nonsense. Occasional déjà vu does not make me the reincarnation of your saint."

"You have dreadlocks, and she had long, thick white-blonde ringlets."

"Fine, she had similar hair. So what? It means nothing. If I was walking around with a black pixie cut, no one would look twice at me."

"You are thinking about this wrong, darling."

"What do you mean?"

"Why do you wear your hair in dreadlocks?" she asked.

"I don't know. Because I like it."

"But why do you like it? Why this style? It cannot be easy for you, maintaining such hair."

"I just like it. I don't know why."

"Perhaps you like it because you have always liked it. Perhaps because that hair was a decision you made over a lifetime ago. We are all drawn to who we once were. Your dreadlocks resemble Vella's ringlets."

I burst out laughing, but Orchid took my arm again. "I know it is hard to understand, but you'll see once we go inside."

"If you say so," I said. "Lead the way."

"I know you are nervous, and I was nervous too the first time I came to the convent. You know, I came the same way you did. I was at the school. I heard the bells, and I wandered down the beach one day. Something drew me here. I cannot explain it."

"And then what? You just dropped out of college and joined the Black Mariahs?"

"Yes," she replied. "When I walked through those

convent doors, I felt like I had come home." She indicated to the two wrought iron doors in front of us.

Rather disconcertingly, they swung open the moment we approached.

"Cameras?" I asked.

"We are not that fancy. Lauriana opened it for us. See?" She waved in the direction of the porch where another Black Mariah leaned over the balcony.

"Hola," the Black Mariah called out. "Bienvenida, Piper!"

I waved back awkwardly and nearly tripped on the flagstone step. Orchid grabbed my elbow to keep me from falling. "Sorry," I said. "This is my first visit to a convent. I don't really know what to expect."

"I am sure you have noticed by now we are not your average nuns."

"I've had very little to do with average nuns, let alone this version of them."

"Don't worry. You have friends here already," she said and stepped across the threshold. I followed her and found myself standing in the middle of a smoky cloud in an incredibly lavish hallway. Everything was made of crystal and mirrors. The floors, the ceilings, and the wall panels were all mirrored glass, and hanging on the glass were silver gilded frames, holding even more mirrors. Majestic chandeliers dropped from the vaulted ceiling. I coughed a little as a nauseating smell of incense assaulted my nose and eyes.

"Well, it's certainly sparkly in here," I said.

Orchid looked pleased. "It's quite something, isn't it? This is my favorite room, even if it is a hallway."

"It's something all right. Especially if one enjoys funhouses."

"Funhouses?"

"Never mind."

"It is modeled after the great Hall of Mirrors in Versailles. Do you know Versailles?" she asked.

"Only from books." The irony of Marie Antoinette and the guillotine was not lost on me.

"You can give her a full tour later," called a voice from the other end of the hall. It was unlike any voice I had ever heard before. Rich and lilting, it was uniquely its own and completely unforgettable. Orchid and I turned toward the sound as a nun stepped out of the shadows. Her black gown touched the floor and shimmered with embellished crystals. Around her neck was the diamond cross choker. I didn't need an introduction.

Malfaedra.

She glided over to us and kissed Orchid on both cheeks. "Darling," she said, "thank you for bringing Piper."

"It was my pleasure, Malfaedra," Orchid said and bowed.

Malfaedra turned to me, her eyes enhanced by dark-purple eye shadow and black eyeliner. She looked like how I pictured Cleopatra if Cleopatra were living in modern times and happened to join a convent.

"Piper," Malfaedra said in her breathless voice. She kissed me on both cheeks too. "I cannot tell you how welcome you are here. I am delighted you came to visit."

"Thank you," I stammered. Her ultra-feminine confidence was so intimidating, I felt at a loss for words.

"Are you hungry? Orchid said you would join us for dinner."

I looked at Orchid, who nodded encouragingly. "Yes, dinner would be nice. Thank you."

Malfaedra turned to Orchid. "Orchid, darling, do you want to dine with us or the others?"

I hoped Orchid would stay with us, but she demurred. "I had a late lunch," she said. "Besides, I have work to do."

"Very well, run along then. Gracias, darling."

Orchid smiled at me, and then skipped off into the shadows of the mirrored hallway. I wondered exactly what Orchid did for work. Pray? Apply more makeup?

"She is a wonderful girl," Malfaedra said. "I am so glad you have made the pleasure of her acquaintance."

I couldn't help but raise my eyebrows at her remark. Orchid dressed up as a housekeeper, broke into my room, and then crept up on me at the pool. I wasn't sure that exactly counted as *making the pleasure of my acquaintance.*

"There is nothing to fear, Piper," she said.

"Nothing for you, perhaps."

"True. I understand."

"You do?"

"I do. This is an island of intrigues. It always has been."

"I only came here for the language program," I said.

Malfaedra's violet eyes narrowed ever so slightly. "I'm sure you will find that is not quite true. Did Orchid explain things to you?"

"In a way."

"And what do you think?"

"About reincarnation, you mean?"

"Precisely. Good, I am glad she spoke to you of the gift."

"Yes, but I came here accidentally. I won an essay. I'd honestly never heard of Carabajel before."

"There are no accidents."

"But I swear—"

"Come with me," she interrupted. "It is my hope what I will show you will change everything."

She led me down the Hall of Mirrors, which did little to calm my nerves. Some of the mirrors were tilted forward on the wall, making the funhouse effect worse on my already shaky legs. I glanced at my reflection and promptly lost my balance.

"Are you all right?" Malfaedra asked.

"Yes," I said, feeling ridiculous that I couldn't walk in a straight line down a hall. But the incense was starting to overwhelm me.

"These mirrors can be difficult to walk next to, but we cannot change them. They hold an exquisite purpose, you know." I waited for her to say something more, but she only smiled mischievously.

I wondered what Julian would say if he knew I was walking alongside Malfaedra into the depths of their towering fortress. Part of me felt bold and empowered. He might even be impressed by my bravery and my willingness to see into their cloistered world. The other part of me—the part that still, unbelievably, trusted him —felt idiotic. *They are dangerous and not dangerous.*

We came to a black lacquered door with an ornamented silver knob in the center. Next to the door was a side table shaped like a half moon and painted the color of ebony. On top of it, a silver candelabra held long, thin black candles.

Malfaedra opened the drawer of the table and removed a cigarette holder, a silver case, and a matching lighter with a row of crystals around its center. She opened the case and offered it to me, but I shook my head. I was way too flustered to attempt smoking.

Malfaedra took one for herself and set the cigarette into the holder. She lit it and rather carelessly dropped the little lighter and case back into the drawer. As she lifted her hand up to hold the cigarette, the sleeve of her gown slid down her arm and I saw she had the same tattoo as Orchid etched into her wrist.

Malfaedra inhaled deeply then said, "Piper, what I am going to show you might be shocking. Sometimes the gift is difficult to accept. It changes one instantly and even the strongest amongst us are unable to reject its powers."

I felt myself nod. Whatever it was she needed to show me, I wanted to get it over with. The incense was really starting to make me feel woozy. It felt like it was choking me, like I was practically eating it.

"Follow me," she said. She pushed open the lacquered door, and I stepped into a room filled with so many purple flowers I thought someone had died. I was so entranced by the fragrant beauty I didn't see the portrait hanging above the fireplace between two flaming sconces. But when I did, I gasped and stepped backward against the door Malfaedra had closed behind me.

The Portrait

The walls of the room were filled with art. Exquisite paintings of landscapes and seascapes hung in more gilded silver frames, and between them were portraits of beautiful women, all wearing the habit of the Black Mariahs. But it was the centerpiece of the room that astounded me. High above the black marble fireplace, with all the lamps in the room casting a spotlight directly on the face, was a grand portrait of me.

Or at least it looked exactly like me. The features were unequivocally the same. The widely spaced eyes, the heart-shaped face, the downward turn of my lips that sometimes made it look like I was wearing a permanent pout. But in place of my dreadlocks were white-blonde banana curls just like Orchid had described.

The woman in the portrait looked older than me, and her haughty expression was certainly one I never sported. But if someone had dressed me in the Black Mariah outfit, put a cross around my neck, and told me to do my best impression of Aisling, I probably could have pulled off a flawless replica. I had to admit that it suddenly made perfect sense why the islanders jumped when they saw me. The resemblance was truly uncanny.

"She is Santa Vella, our late high priestess," Malfaedra said evenly. "Now you understand, child, why you are attracting so much attention here. And why you are also in danger."

"But it still doesn't mean anything," I whispered. "Lots of people look like people. In the States, people make a fortune because they look like someone else. Look at all of the Elvis impersonators."

"Sit down," she commanded gently. She motioned toward a velvet lavender sofa and then took a seat across from me in a matching tufted chair. "You want to believe this is an accident? A miracle of genetics, perhaps?"

"Yes."

"Piper, as I said before, there are no accidents. We have waited for you for a very long time."

"But I won an essay contest that brought me here. I only entered the contest because I didn't feel like spending the summer in New Jersey."

"And you do not think that was fate?"

"No, I think I got lucky and won a contest."

"Then how do you explain the Incurable?"

"I'm sorry, the what?"

"You were with your friend. You walked to the Incurable and uncovered the old staircase to Carabajel. How did you know it was there?"

"I still don't know what you mean by the Incurable." But I did know. The ruins of the gothic church. The shortcut to downtown.

"The dysentery church," Malfaedra said. "No one walks down that road. No one. It is the church where the poor incurables were sent to die until Vella found the cure."

"But," I protested, "it was an accident I found the church. My friend and I were walking to dinner."

The superior look on her face told me she was taking note of my discomfort. "I told you already, Piper, there are no accidents."

"How did you know I was on that road?" I asked even though the answer was obvious. The general had watchers. The Black Mariahs probably did too.

"There is no privacy on Carabajel," she replied. "And certainly not in the old quarter. Only here on these grounds are you safe from prying eyes. Piper, it all becomes easier when you stop resisting. Was this island not familiar to you when you arrived? Have you not been walking around feeling a peculiar sensation of having been here before?"

I knew what she was saying was true. Every time the déjà vu hit me it had been like reliving a vague memory. I wanted to lie to her. I wanted to tell her again I knew nothing about anything, to maintain I was an average, uninteresting kid with plans to go to Vassar and no real goals after that because Vassar always seemed like a goal unto itself.

I looked down at my hands and then back at Malfaedra. I wanted to trust her, yet a much bigger part of me wanted to trust Julian, even if he had proved to be the liar of the century.

"I don't understand," I said. It was a statement that made no sense, but it bought me some time.

"I know. It is difficult to accept. For some of us, knowing our past is a comfort our souls will live again. But in your case, the gift of reincarnation means so much more."

"Why?"

"You came looking for us, didn't you?"

"A coincidence," I said.

"Was it?" Malfaedra asked. Her violet eyes were blinding.

"I don't know. Maybe I do look like her. But do all of you come back looking like you did the first time around? It must make for a very redundant portrait gallery."

Malfaedra ignored my cynicism. "It is important for you to understand Vella's story. Will you listen, Piper?"

"Um, okay," I said, although I suspected I did not have much choice.

She leaned forward, her face gleaming with excitement. She lowered her voice as though there were others in the room. "It was Vella who uncovered the magic of Carabajel's volcanic ash. You see, she was Icelandic. She was born in the Land of Ice and Fire."

"She was from Iceland?" I didn't know why that was interesting, but it was, perhaps because I found it unfathomable a woman from an island near the Arctic Circle would come to mean so much to an island in the Caribbean.

Malfaedra nodded. "Yes, she studied horticulture and volcanology before joining the convent. She knew flowers. She understood the mystery of plants like no other. She developed the medicine that cured the dysentery outbreak. And she mastered the cultivation of the black sugar cane."

"I thought the general discovered the black sugar."

Malfaedra shook her head. "It was all Vella. The discovery, the methodology for growing the sugar cane in the ash, and the plans for exportation. The general and his soldiers were once our guards before the fools we are stuck with now, so of course they were privy to our secrets. Once the exportation of the sugar changed our finances, we were no longer reliant on the Vatican's funds. We overthrew their control, and then the general and his men overthrew us. It's a story as old as time."

I thought of Coco's comment about the saints in the book not being Catholic. "I don't understand how the Vatican fits in here," I said.

Malfaedra extinguished her cigarette into a little silver ashtray and then reached into a drawer in the end table next to the sofa and pulled out another one. She lit it and leaned back and exhaled.

"The Vatican owned this island. For centuries they would send their internal dissenters here. Anyone who was a risk to their teachings."

She tapped the ashes of her cigarette into the ashtray. "You see, Piper, until two decades ago, Carabajel was an unknown island. You can imagine how easy it was for the Vatican to hide it from the world. Now it is impossible. The Internet has changed everything, even if we do not quite utilize its technology here."

"I guess that makes sense."

"Apparently, it is the general's theory that by further opening Carabajel, it will ensure his survival. How ironic it will actually bring his destruction."

"His destruction?" I echoed.

"The general had Vella killed, and when he did, she left behind a prophecy, a warning, you could say. And do you know what it was?"

I shook my head, and she folded her arms across her chest. Her diamond ring flickered in the light of the fire and cast a rainbow-like glow across the wall behind her.

"When I return, you will die," Malfaedra said.

"Who will die?"

"The general first then all of his loyalists. I must admit, as the years passed, we stopped believing the prophecy. You see, our gifts are about the past, not the future. But then you appeared. Suddenly, like a specter, there you were, standing before me on the beach, flinging a little rock into the sea."

Malfaedra stood up, went to the mantle, and opened a small metal box encrusted with jewels. She pulled out a handful of something I couldn't see and clutched it thoughtfully in her fist before tossing it into the fire. I watched as the flames turned from red to a bright blue and then purple. The fire began smoking deeply, and the smell of incense increased exponentially.

"You will understand once you spend more time with us," she said. "In the meantime, we must be careful. You are a great danger for that sorry excuse of a general. He will go to any length to destroy you before you destroy him. With our help, of course."

"That's absurd," I said. "No one is getting destroyed because I'm not Vella." Yet as I spoke, I realized everything was finally coming together. The Carabajelians knew about the prophecy too, which explained why everyone looked at me with dread. Julian had said Vella's legend was reaching critical mass. And the taxi driver had said the end was near. And then there was Clara. No wonder she almost passed out when she saw me sitting at his dining table. Obviously, she was loyal to the Black Mariahs because she was in possession of their rosary. She must have been worried the general was going to have me killed that very night, and she tried to tell me to go to the nuns.

But something was bothering me about the general. He'd been so nice. Why didn't he just kill me then and there? I was sitting right at his dining room table. He could have pretended there was an accident. Or had he planned to kill me and somehow his plot had been foiled? The fact I could have been murdered made me cold with fear.

"Well?" Malfaedra asked. "What do you think?"

I struggled to find the right words. "I will say," I began and stopped. I tried again. "I will concede some things are..." I was about to say "familiar" when the door burst open. A man entered the room wearing the uniform of either a security guard or a doorman or maybe both. Perhaps he was a security guard who opened doors. Either way, he had on a blue double-breasted suit with silver buttons and a matching hat.

"Samuel!" Malfaedra shrieked. "How dare you enter

without knocking?"

"My apologies, priestess. There is an emergency."

"Go on."

"Observadores on the hill."

"How many?" she asked.

"Four."

"Are they armed?"

"Yes. We have captured two of them, priestess. We are holding them at the east crossing."

Malfaedra sighed with disgust. "I will have to pay them a visit personally, won't I?"

She turned back to me. "Piper, darling, wait here a few moments. I will send for Orchid to keep you company. It has been years since the general sent his watchers down here. Apparently, they are in need of a reminder as to why they should never march onto our grounds."

She bent down and lifted her gown ever so slightly, removing a tiny pearl-handled pistol from a strap on her black ankle boot.

"Fernando will escort you, priestess," Samuel said.

Samuel walked past me to a door by the fireplace I had not noticed before. He swung it open, and the tropical sea air gusted in refreshingly.

But the sea air was followed by another scent. A very recognizable scent.

Standing on the porch was a large man wearing the same uniform as Samuel, the tip of his cigar flickering brightly. He gazed at me before holding out his arm for Malfaedra.

The Hall of Mirrors

I averted my eyes and stared straight into the fireplace. My heart started pounding so hard, I was certain everyone in the room could hear it. I was positive it was the same type of cigar I had smelled outside my dorm. Which meant the man who had been stalking me and Coco was one of the Black Mariahs' guards. I had convinced myself he had been linked to the general. Maybe Malfaedra had ordered him to guard me, but there was still the matter of the exterior lights being extinguished. And I was sure I had seen a knife. An instinct deep inside me was telling me something was amiss.

I sat there mutely as the three of them disappeared outside. The door slammed shut followed by the sound of a lock clicking into place. I wondered if Malfaedra had forgotten her plan to send Orchid to keep me company.

I clenched my hands together. I wanted to escape, but even if I managed to get out of the convent, I was certain there was no way I could get to the beach gate without being seen.

I had come to the convent for answers, and until Samuel burst through the door, I had been quite certain I had found what I was looking for. Putting the reincarnation bit aside because I still wasn't quite buying it, at least I understood what the whole fuss was about. I was a dead ringer for Vella, who was apparently a gardening star and who found a way to grow medicinal herbs that saved the Carabajelians from dysentery. She also managed to cultivate a black sugar that brought everyone riches. The general staged a coup and killed her, and the Carabajelians hated him for what he had done. If you left the prophecy bit out of the mix, the story sounded rather logical.

I couldn't help but wonder what Fernando had been doing at my dorm. My sinking suspicion was that Malfaedra didn't like my vague response to Orchid's dinner invitation, so she tried another tactic and sent Fernando after me. He probably would have dragged me to the convent, but he couldn't because I was with Coco. But now what was Malfaedra planning to do with me? Brainwash me and convert me to the Black Mariahs? Everything made sense and nothing made sense.

I have got to get out of here, I thought. If I could get back to the main doors, I might be able to hide outside until darkness when I could make a run for the beach. It was risky, but the way I saw it, I didn't have much choice. I mustered up all the courage I had and stood up. If any of the nuns caught me in the hallway, I could always say I was looking for a ladies' room.

I tiptoed across the room toward the door leading to the Hall of Mirrors. Before I turned the knob, I took one last look at the portrait of Vella and winced. It was the eeriest thing I had ever seen. I couldn't resist pulling out my phone and snapping a picture. Someday, I thought, I would need proof all of this really happened.

I tried to open the door quietly, but it still creaked a little on its hinges. The incense continued to burn somewhere, overpowering the entire hallway with a smoky haze. I could hear music playing, a low chanting that sounded very much like the same sound I always heard at the street party.

I stepped into the hall and pinned myself back against the doorframe, then looked in both directions. It was empty, but I chided myself for being a total idiot. If I really had to use a bathroom, would I be stepping into the hallway like a CIA operative?

I walked about a hundred steps down the hallway. I

was quite certain the incense cloud had thickened. I tried not to gag, but the smoke was unbearable. I looked up at the ceiling, trying to figure out where it was coming from. Were they pumping it in from somewhere?

I reached out and touched the wall alongside me, and I felt the edge of one of the gilded mirrors. But where was the door? All I remembered was Orchid and I had stepped into the hallway, and then Malfaedra had appeared out of nowhere. I'd been so nervous I hadn't paid attention to how far we had walked before Malfaedra opened the door to the parlor.

And hadn't Malfaedra said something about the mirrors being there for a reason? Was it because they were doors? I ran my fingers along the edges, trying to find something like a hinge or a way to slide them open. Then it dawned on me. One of the houses we had lived in had a mirrored medicine cabinet in the bathroom that you had to press on to get it to release. I looked at the tallest mirror closest to me and pushed firmly on the edge.

Nothing.

Okay, don't panic, they can't all be doors, I told myself. I inched farther until I found another high one and pressed firmly in the approximate area where you would expect a doorknob. A mechanical click sounded, and the mirror released from the wall. I couldn't believe I had actually figured it out.

I pulled the door open cautiously and tried to turn my face into a mask of stupidity. If the door led to a room full of Black Mariahs, I would just pretend I was high on incense. But I was greeted by nothing more than an empty room filled with church pews, candelabras, and an altar with a statue of a woman behind it. The altar looked to be made of amethyst, and surrounding it were black candles that had been burning so long, the wax had created stalactites that almost reached the floor.

I backed out of the room and then recalled Orchid and I had walked through wrought iron doors, not mirrored panels. But where were those doors? Or had I gone down a different hallway? I wanted to beat my head against the altar.

"Piper, is that you?"

I turned to see the faint outline of Orchid moving through the haze.

"Yes, it's just me," I replied, my heartbeat quickening.

"That was a quick meeting," she said.

"Um, yes, it was." I hoped I was not about to get caught in a lie. Malfaedra had left less than ten minutes before, headed to some crossing. I prayed Orchid had not intercepted her.

"Aren't you staying for dinner?" she asked.

"I think Malfaedra had to take care of something. One of your security guards came to talk to her."

"Oh, too bad," she said. "I'm sure she'll invite you again, especially now we know you are one of us."

I thought fast. If Orchid could walk me as far as the beach gate, I would be home free. The nun by the doors and the guards on watch couldn't possibly think I was trying to escape if Orchid was with me. It was dicey, but even with Orchid's friendly presence, something was still telling me I had to get out of the convent. And fast.

"I'm sure I will be back," I said. "Listen, do you think you could walk me down to the gate? That ledge is treacherous."

"Of course," Orchid replied. "It is getting dark, though. Are you sure you don't want one of the guards to drive you back?"

"No," I said a little too quickly. "I mean, no, that's not necessary. I think they are busy anyway. Something about observers at the east crossing."

"Really? How odd."

"Is it odd?"

She nodded. "They haven't sent people here for years. I wonder if it has something to do with you. The general must be getting nervous."

More than anything, I wanted to ask her to elaborate, but I knew it was only a matter of time before Malfaedra came back, and I really didn't relish walking the strip of beach in the darkness. I looked at my watch and grimaced. How had the time passed so quickly? It was almost seven forty-five.

"Sorry, where are the doors?" I asked.

"Just down there," she replied. "How ever did you end up in the chapel?"

"I was blinded by the incense."

She laughed as she led me a few feet in the opposite direction. The wrought iron doors had been just steps away from me the entire time.

Orchid pushed the doors open, and I was so relieved to actually be able to breathe in fresh air and not the sickening aroma. The nun watching the entryway, Lorraine or Lauriana, leaned over the porch railing and waved to us again.

I looked up at the sky. It was darker than I would have liked. The moon was out, but it was almost entirely hidden by clouds. I was going to have to run all the way back to the dorm. At least I could take some comfort in the fact I had identified the cigar stalker, and I knew he was with Malfaedra somewhere else at the moment.

"Are you sure you don't want a car to bring you home?" she asked again, her stilettos clicking on the granite steps. "I can easily get someone to drive you. It's pretty dark out here."

"Thanks, I'm good." I smiled as though I always walked down beaches at nightfall. "I really want some time to reflect on everything. You know, the gift."

She nodded. "I completely understand. We always take time for reflection." Then she pointed to the waves. Their spray was almost reaching the top of the ledge. "My, my, look at those breakers. I hardly ever see them reach the top of the ledge."

"I better hurry," I told her.

"Maybe you can come back tomorrow. I'll ask Malfaedra, but I'm sure it will be fine."

"Sure. I'll even bring my makeup bag," I joked, but when her face lit up, I felt bad. I turned away from her and clung to the banister as I climbed the spiral steps. When I reached the top, I waved, and she waved back as though we were the best of friends.

I couldn't imagine her life as my own, locked away from the world forever.

⚝ 24 ⚝

Race Against the Sea

I gulped as I closed the gate behind me and looked down at the beach. The tide was so alarmingly high, it was already flowing into the mangroves. I didn't mind getting my feet wet, but if I didn't get a move on there was going to be no beach left at all.

As my feet hit the sand and I started to run, I thought about Orchid and I felt a few pangs of guilt. I hoped she didn't get into trouble for unknowingly escorting me off the convent grounds when Malfaedra had ordered me to wait.

I heard a rushing noise and jumped to my left to avoid a wave that broke way too close to the beach for my liking. My arms and the side of my face scraped against a harsh branch of the underbrush, and I felt a trickle of blood drip down my arm. I stopped for a second to catch my breath even though I knew I was running out of time. That wave had been colossal. Way too colossal. Then I remembered the storm.

The only hurricane I had experienced had been in New Jersey when we first arrived on base. It had been a mild one, just a Category One or Two, but I recalled the tide had surged so far inland, the water had reached the boardwalk and covered the porch of the Humpty Dumpty.

My body was telling me to slow down and rest, but my brain was telling me to pick up the pace. I listened to my brain and started to run again. I strained my eyes to see any indication of the lights of the school, but the only thing in front of me was a wall of darkness. Whatever happened to the moon? I looked up at the sky, but even the stars were gone.

I silently cursed every curse I could think of. It was the bloody Fourth of July. I should be eating clam cakes and watching the fireworks after the base air show. Instead, what was I doing? Running down a flooding beach with a cult of nuns on my tail.

Finally, unless my eyes were deceiving me, I saw a light flickering up ahead. It had to be the spotlight on the top of the administration building. In my excitement, I stumbled as my feet sank in the damp sand. Water rushed past me, its force pitching me face first into the swirling surf. As I struggled to pull myself up again, a sliver of moonlight broke through the blackness.

"Holy Mother!" I exclaimed. The waves were gigantic, bigger than any of the ones I'd seen in Jersey. They were high and foaming, one right behind the other as though they were in a race to get to the beach.

I tried to remember everything my father had taught me about survival. What had he said to do about the sea? All I could remember was to wait half an hour after eating before going for a swim and to swim sideways if I got caught in a riptide. But neither piece of advice applied at the moment. In this instance, he would probably tell me to run for my life, and that was exactly what I was going to do. Don't look, don't look, I coached myself. Just run.

The school was coming into sight and I squinted to see the seawall. Wasn't there a fixed maintenance ladder somewhere that led to the top? I was sure I had seen it before. The path to the pool from the beach was at least a hundred yards away, and I wasn't going to make it. I had no choice but to try to find the ladder or the waves were going to crush me against the concrete. I held my left hand out to feel for the wall and tried to run on my toes so my feet wouldn't sink into the sand. Two more waves crashed around me before cold, bumpy stucco scraped my open palm.

I prayed I had not passed the ladder. I wasn't sure how much of the wall I had missed, and even though my eyes had adjusted to the darkness, it was like I was running in a cave.

Wild spray showered over me, and I coughed as salt-water got into my mouth and nose. Then, just as I lost my balance again, my fingers grazed the metal edge of the ladder. I sighed with relief and grasped the first slippery rung. I held on for dear life as a wave smacked into me, its force smothering me.

As soon as it went out to sea again, I reached up and made it a few more rungs before another wave crashed against me. The water was rising so high against the wall, it was nearly at my waist.

I pulled myself up three more rungs to the top. As I swung my legs over the seawall, the next wave exploded behind me knocking me right off the wall onto the cement path. I lay there for a second, trying to catch my breath. The general and the Black Mariahs felt like kittens compared to the ocean.

Then I had a horrifying thought that the whole wall might give in. I dragged myself to my feet and ran again until I reached the manicured grass of the campus. There was a flagpole in front of me, and I leaned against it to rest. At the top of the pole, flapping in the wind, were two square red-and-black flags, one hanging right above the other. Hurricane warning.

I looked down at my clothes. They were soaked through and covered in sand. My purse was waterlogged and dripping like a wet balloon. I knew I should get back to my room, shower, and dry off before I started to shiver, but I was so exhausted, I wanted to drop onto the grass and go to sleep.

Put one foot in front of the other, I told myself. Think of a hot shower and bed. I couldn't remember if Cecilia had said something about homework. I had been so fixated on visiting the convent, it felt like class ended days ago, not mere hours. I considered knocking on Coco's door to ask her what I was supposed to be working on, but I quickly decided against it. After my hair-raising evening, I deserved a break from homework.

Homework. It was the one thing throughout my life I had always been diligent about, especially once I got to high school and grade-point average mattered. I wasn't smart in the never-having-to-study kind of way. I worked for every single grade "A" I got. I studied for every test, especially the standardized ones. I knew I had to if I ever wanted to get away from the Air Force.

For so long, I had focused on Vassar because I always thought it was the type of place a girl could go to ensure she would make something of her life, even if I didn't know what that something was. In that regard, Coco was way more advanced than me. She knew she wanted to be in fashion and that was that.

I bent down and pulled off my sandals. Damn Vassar, I thought, and damn me for not having realistic goals. Maybe my father was right about me pursuing something more practical like nursing or teaching. If I'd listened to him, I wouldn't be half dead, tangled up in a mess with nuns and generals, and now a hurricane to boot.

Hi Dad, I would say if I could get the pay phone to work. *Yeah, you were right about the international relations major thing. I'd like to come home early, please. Oh, and by the way, it appears as though I might be reincarnated. I used to be a nun. And could you hurry up with a plane ticket? At least one, if not two, of the warring factions on the island are trying to kill me.*

As I got closer to the octagon dorms, I peeked around a palm tree to see if any of my classmates were in the lobby lounge. Sure enough, even with the rising wind and rolling surf, I could hear the unmistakable sound of their laughter. I really, really did not want to have to explain myself, so I backed up and walked toward the opposite side of the building. I doubted anyone would be there as long as the spray was still breaking over the top of the seawall.

I hugged the side of the building, walked around it to the front, and then started across the parking lot toward the staircase closest to my room. It wasn't until I reached the top step that I realized once again all the exterior lights were off. I stopped short and felt myself tremble. Did I dare try to make it to my room alone? But if I didn't, I would have to tell everyone why I was soaked and covered in sand.

I stuck my head out of the stairwell to look around. Just as I did, a beam from a flashlight to my right blinded me, and a man wearing black rushed toward me. I screamed right before I lost my footing and fell backward down the steps.

Then I heard a familiar voice call my name.

Julian.

25

The Prophecy

As I tumbled down, I managed to grab the banister on the stairwell, but not before I smashed my right temple against something cold and metallic. The sudden sharp pain and the rush of warm blood did me in. I toppled onto the steps in a heap.

"Piper, dios mio!" Julian exclaimed. From the top step, he stared at my crumpled state in horror.

I wanted to laugh at the hilarity of the whole scene, but my head was throbbing so badly, I couldn't do or say anything.

Julian dashed down the steps to where I was sitting. He tore off his sweatshirt and pressed it with force against the gash. I tried not to focus on the pain, but I was seeing stars.

"Are you out of your mind?" he asked.

"Out of my mind? I fell. Do you think I did it on purpose?"

"I never know what you are doing!"

The blood was now dripping down my arm, and the flashlight he was shining in my eyes was getting on my last nerve. "Obviously, I hit my head on the wall."

"You are covered in blood and...are those twigs?"

"Probably. Look, if you plan on criticizing my appearance, you could at least move the flashlight out of my eyes."

Julian blinked. "What? Oh, sorry."

"I went out for a long walk and then a jog. And, um, Julian?"

"Yes?"

The walls were beginning to sway in a circle. "I think I'm going to faint."

"Don't panic," he instructed. "It's not too bad. Heads bleed a lot. I need to apply this pressure for a little longer. We need to get it bandaged too. Do you have bandages in your room?"

"Seriously? Of course not."

"I'm so sorry you fell, Piper," he said.

"Liar," I managed back. My voice was a mere squeak from all the saltwater I had swallowed.

"No, I really didn't mean to make you fall."

"Not about that. You are a liar about other things."

"What are you talking about?"

"You go to school here, huh? Live in the dorm over yonder."

He was silent for a second, and then he leaned back and sighed. "Yes, about that. Okay, I am a liar. But I am in a pre-med program. At the University of Costa Rica. I can explain."

"Get away from me."

"I'm not leaving you like this. Besides, I came here because there are a few things I need to talk to you about. Starting with where the hell were you last night?"

"None of your business."

"It is my business, Piper."

"Yeah, why?"

"You know why."

"I said get away from me and I meant it."

"No." He leaned over the top of my head again. "Do you think you can walk? If we go to your room, I can bandage it properly. I am actually planning to be a doctor."

"Shocking."

"I swear. Piper, I am so sorry, really."

"Okay, okay. But I want an explanation." I thought of Malfaedra and the threat against his father. "And I need to tell you a few things myself."

"Let's go then. Try to stand." He reached under my arm and helped me up.

We started up the steps very slowly until we were back on the third floor. Then we both jumped because Aisling and Gareth were standing on the threshold to Aisling's room. They looked from me to Julian and back to me again.

"Piper, are you all right?" Aisling asked.

"Never better." I tried to smile.

"Are you sure?" Gareth asked. He looked skeptical and glared at Julian as though Julian had beaten me.

"She fell down the stairs," Julian said.

"It wasn't his fault. I didn't expect to see him in the hall, and I slipped backward."

Aisling folded her arms and leaned against the doorway. "Then why are you all wet and covered in mud?"

"It's sand," I replied. Of all times for them to start acting like hall monitors. "I fell in the saltwater pool and it was really rough. I had a hard time getting out."

Julian exchanged glances with me. He knew I was lying.

"Stay away from the saltwater pool, Piper," Gareth said. "Hurricane Lila is due to strike as early as tomorrow afternoon."

"Perfect. Gareth, maybe you should rethink the engineering thing and go into meteorology."

"Yes, thank you very much for the weather update," Julian said a tad sarcastically, but Gareth missed it and beamed.

"Piper, are you sure you're okay?" Aisling asked. I was touched and surprised by her concern.

"Yes," I replied. "Thanks."

"As long as you're sure. Have a good night then."

"You too," I said. "See you tomorrow."

Aisling blew me a kiss, pushed Gareth back inside her room, and closed her door.

Julian was holding on tight to my arm, and with his other hand, he was still pressing his sweatshirt against the back of my head. "Let's go," he said. "I need to wrap your head."

When we got to my door, I fumbled in my purse for my keys and handed them to Julian. I couldn't believe they had not fallen out when I tripped in the sand. I was relieved my journal was still inside my purse too, even if it was all puffed up from being waterlogged.

Julian unlocked the door and then ordered me to sit down on the edge of my bed. I was too exhausted to care that my room still looked as though someone had set off a grenade.

"Let me take a look," he said.

"Ow," I mumbled when he touched the wound.

"It hurts?"

"Yeah, but whatever, I'm fine."

"You don't have to be so strong you know."

"It was stupid to trip the way I did."

"It really isn't too bad, even though it was bleeding a

lot. I think you actually hit the edge of the fire extinguisher box, which is why you got cut."

"Oh," I said. "I didn't see it."

"You couldn't have. All of the lights were out. Do you know why?"

I shook my head. "Do you?"

"No, but it is cause for concern. I was glad I had the flashlight. Have they been out for a while?"

"Last night and tonight."

"Very suspicious. Look, I'm going to run down to the lobby and get some bandages. I suggest you take a hot shower but be careful of the wound."

When he left, I locked the door behind him and bolted it. I could have given him the keys, but I didn't exactly like the idea of him letting himself back in while I was in the shower. I still wasn't sure I should trust him, and I wasn't about to leave it open should Fernando happen to make a reappearance.

By now, Malfaedra definitely knew I had escaped. What if she sent him after me again? I didn't want to admit it aloud, but secretly I was glad Julian was with me. I hadn't exactly analyzed the long-term consequences of me disappearing from the convent.

I turned the shower on and peeled off my drenched clothes. When the water finally got hot, I stepped into the tub and let the scalding heat warm my body. I had to somehow muster up the energy to interrogate Julian. I knew this was my moment to get answers, but all I really wanted to do was crawl into bed and knock myself out with aspirin.

After my shower, I pulled on my nightshirt and pinned my dreadlocks up in a bun. I also emptied the contents of my purse into the sink and, with the exception of my journal and my phone, I rinsed everything out, including my change purse. My eyeliner rolled toward the drain, and I couldn't help wincing again over the image of Orchid waving goodbye to me at the beach gate.

When Julian returned, I demanded he say his name twice before I opened the door. I wasn't taking any chances.

He came in with a handful of bandages and a bottle of antiseptic. He cleaned the gash with a tissue from the bathroom and placed a bandage over it.

His sweatshirt was crumpled up in a ball next to me. "Sorry," I said, pointing to it. "It looks like you slaughtered someone."

"Of all things to apologize for. I still can't believe you fell down the stairs right in front of me. I thought you cracked your skull open when I saw all that blood."

"No such luck."

"Piper?"

"Yes?"

He sat down in the desk chair and faced me. "I need to ask why you went to the convent. Do you know how insane that was? I told you the nuns are dangerous."

"I think you technically said they are both 'dangerous and not dangerous.' I thought maybe this was one of the not dangerous times."

"Piper—"

"Now it's my turn. Why don't we start with why you lied to me about living at the school?"

"All right, fine. I needed a reason to be in the library and it was a plausible lie. When I said it, I thought we would never see each other again. But then I couldn't stop thinking about you, so I asked you out. I planned to tell you over dinner, but you took off like a rocket, remember?"

I crossed my arms. "Why did you need a plausible reason to be at the library?"

"My father sent me to, well, check up on you."

"So, you were spying on me? I knew it! And you acted like I was an idiot for thinking you were in there stalking me."

"I'm sorry."

"Then tell me why your father sent you to follow me."

"Piper, please hear me out. I was supposed to run into you accidentally and talk to you for five minutes and then go back and report. That was it. The walk we took, the dinner, everything beyond that was not on the agenda."

"What agenda?"

"Listen, please," he begged. "When my father asked

me about the Vella imposter, I told him it was true and that I even caught a glimpse of her, you, downtown. He was very disturbed. He demanded I have a quick chat with you to find out what you were all about."

"And did you? Did you find out what I was 'all about'?"

"No, of course not. But I learned you weren't connected to the Black Mariahs or someone playing a prank."

"And that's what you reported back?"

"Yes. I reported you looked exactly like every image of Santa Vella I had ever seen, but you were seemingly oblivious about Carabajel."

A thought popped into my head and I narrowed my eyes. "You are lying again," I said.

"I'm not!"

"You forgot I had already met your father the day before the library incident. Remember, he invited me to your palace. We had coffee. He was nice to me. I don't understand why he sent you to investigate me after he had already met me."

"I didn't know when I met you in the library that you had already met him."

"Your father didn't tell you?"

"No. That was why I was so shocked when I found out. As soon as I got back to the palace, I insisted he tell me why he had been deceptive."

"And?" I asked.

"And he said he wanted me to investigate you without any preconceived notions. He was truly worried about your safety."

"How nice," I fumed. "Funny, the nuns said the exact same thing."

"His fear was that Malfaedra was going to hypnotize you and bring you into the convent as one of their own. He said he couldn't deal with the publicity if an American went missing. Remember, Carabajel is newly open to tourists. A scandal like that could kill what little tourism we have."

"Tourism should be killed off. This island is hell on earth. And then why did you even ask me out? You could have left me alone."

"Because I couldn't get you out of my mind no matter how hard I tried. I thought you were funny and smart, and I'd never met anyone like you before."

I just glared at him. Flattery was not going to work.

"Piper, you still haven't told me what made you go to the convent today."

"How did you find out?"

"You even have to ask? My father has you under surveillance, but we lost track of you last night. Or rather I lost track of you much to my father's annoyance. Where were you?"

"In Coco's room. She's one of my classmates."

"But I told you I was going to come over last night. Did you forget?"

"No. I didn't want to see you. I'd just found out about the school being closed down."

"Oh. I see," he said. "I'm sorry again. I was planning to tell you yesterday."

"Yeah, right."

"I was, I swear to you. Who told you anyway? Malfaedra?"

"Actually, no. I ran into a landscaper when I was looking for you. He told me the school has been closed for a couple of years. Then a Black Mariah showed up at the pool and convinced me I could trust them and not you. She invited me for dinner with Malfaedra and I went. So there."

He looked upset, but he nodded anyway. "All right, so you went to the convent and then what happened? My father's men said you made a run for the beach."

"Your father's surveillance can't be that good if you don't know the answer. Last night, a guy was hiding and smoking a cigar in the bushes. I think he made a move to come after me, which is why I slept in Coco's room. Tonight, when I was sitting in Malfaedra's parlor, the same guy was there. It freaked me out, so I took off when no one was looking."

"My God. Of all nights for me to be running late. Do you know who he was?"

"One of Malfaedra's guards. Fernando is his name and his giveaway was his cigar."

"You could have been hurt, Piper. I warned you."

"I know, I know. But it was proving impossible for me to figure out who to trust around here. After I caught you in a lie, I thought I should trust Malfaedra. But I think Fernando had a knife, and I have a feeling if Coco hadn't been with me, he would have grabbed me."

"Exactly! Tonight, my father sent four men to trail you. They were going to get you out if Malfaedra tried anything, but two got caught and the other two saw you take off through the beach gate right before dark. They tried to follow you, but they said the beach was washed away. I raced here when I found out. I hoped, knowing you as I do, a few little waves were not going to deter my Super Doll."

"Yeah, well, I almost didn't make it."

"And your weather friend is right about the hurricane. We will probably call a mandatory evacuation tomorrow from the beach communities and the low-lying areas. You can come to the palace with me. All your friends can come."

"That's so nice of you," I said, though I couldn't quite envision the lot of us hanging out with Julian and the general in the chateau.

"Piper, I need to know something," Julian said. "Did Malfaedra try anything? Hypnotic, I mean?"

"No, but she didn't have time, either. Your men showed up right after I sat down in her parlor. She is burning some serious incense, and I think it has something in it. I felt trippy the whole time I was there."

I rubbed my head where the bandage was. It was starting to throb badly. "I think I need some painkillers," I said.

"Do you have any?" Julian asked.

"Makeup bag in the bathroom."

He went and got it, along with a glass of water. I swallowed two in one gulp. "So why didn't you tell me the whole story when we were at the flamingo restaurant?" I asked. "Or afterward when we were here?"

Julian sat down in the chair again. "Flamenco," he corrected. "I don't know. You had already flipped once. I didn't want to feel your wrath again. It was pretty intense."

"Let me tell you this whole thing gets more intense. The Black Mariahs and apparently most Carabajelians think I'm Vella back from the dead. As in reincarnated. A prophecy come true."

"It's all that superstition nonsense. Malfaedra is crazier than I thought."

"It's not just Malfaedra. All the nuns there believe they are reincarnated. That's why the Vatican sent them here originally. Didn't you know?"

"The Black Mariahs are not exactly my father's favorite dinner conversation topic. All he said was they turned to black magic under Malfaedra. I never gave them a second thought."

"Clara knows something," I said.

"Clara?" He looked confused. "My father's housekeeper?"

"I'll elaborate if you promise she won't get in trouble."

"I can't promise that if she did something."

"I think she might have been trying to warn me, not hurt me. When I went to your house for coffee, she shoved one of the Black Mariahs' rosaries into my hand when your father wasn't looking. She said something that I didn't hear. I think it was 'Santa Vella.' That's the reason I was in the library looking for a book. I was trying to figure it all out."

"I don't know what Clara was doing. I do know the Black Mariahs are maniacal. My father should have shut their convent down years ago. Why he lets them continue to wreak such havoc is beyond me."

"Don't get Clara in trouble and send her to your dungeon."

"Not that again. Okay, fine. But I should ask her what she was doing."

"Wait, there's more," I said.

"Dear God."

"The prophecy. Do you know exactly what it is?"

"Whatever it is, I'm sure it is pure stupidity."

"When Vella died, she said, 'When I return, you will die.' That's the prophecy in a nutshell."

"Well, who was she talking to? Who do they think is going to die?"

"Your father. And his loyalists too."

"That's insane. As if they could ever get to him anyway."

"Malfaedra said Vella was the one who knew the secret of the black sugar, and your father killed her over it. And now Malfaedra seems to think because I am Vella back from the dead it's time for him to die. Don't ask me who is going to do the job. Their plans get a little thin here."

"That is the most ridiculous thing I have ever heard."

"Agreed." I rubbed my temple. How long did it take double aspirin to kick in? Fifteen minutes? Thirty? I prayed it was fifteen.

"Don't touch," Julian said.

"I have a migraine now. Let's blame it on my long day."

"Your long day was your own doing."

"Fair enough." I propped one of my pillows under my elbow and leaned back against it. "Maybe we should go over it again?" I offered.

"No, I've got it down," Julian replied. "Malfaedra thinks my father killed Vella and stole the sugar secret. Now she is ready to enact some twisted revenge because she took one look at you and thinks Vella is back and her prophecy is coming true."

"Pretty much," I said.

"But there is one major problem. My father didn't kill Vella."

"How do you know? I don't want to implicate the guy, but do you think he would admit it to you?"

"Put it this way, the man is incapable of killing a thing. He saves the lives of flies that end up in the palace. A soft heart lurks underneath all his military pageantry. For Christ's sake, the man collects Chinese Cresteds."

"What the hell is a Chinese Crested?"

"A hairless dog."

"That's awful!"

"It's not exactly hairless. It has hair on its feet and its ears."

"All right, all right. Forget the dog. So, despite the fact that everyone on this island is terrified of him, your dad can't kill a bug?"

"Exactly."

"Maybe killing a person is easier than killing a bug."

"Believe me, his tough demeanor is all an act to maintain control. Speaking of him, I've got to tell him you are here safe in your room." He took his satellite phone out of his jeans pocket. "The only problem with this thing is I need to use it outside or else I can't get a signal."

"Use the balcony." I nodded in the direction of the sliding door. The curtains were moving ever so slightly even though the door and windows were shut.

I found out why the second Julian unlocked it and slid the door open. A fierce wind rushed through the open door sending the lamp in the corner crashing to the floor. Julian picked it up and pulled the door closed again. "Jesus, it is really getting bad out there. The wind must be blowing half a gale now. There's no way I will get a connection in these conditions. I don't want to leave you here alone, but I also have to warn my father he could be in more danger than usual if Malfaedra is planning something."

"Maybe he knows already," I said.

"He could. He is a bit vague about his convent years, but he always claimed that once Vella died, Malfaedra became evil.

"Yeah, well, he can say whatever he wants."

"You really think he killed Vella?"

"I hope not, but you have to admit it does look bad. Maybe Vella drank hemlock. Or maybe she inhaled too much volcanic ash. Or caught something at the Incurable. The fact is, no matter how she died, your father was the one who gained the most from her death."

"He didn't kill her."

"Fine, I believe you, but unfortunately, Malfaedra does not. And given these little rebellions that keep popping up, I would say the Carabajelians don't believe him, either."

"I have to talk to him."

"And say what?"

"I don't know. But I have to warn him things may have taken a lethal turn where Malfaedra is concerned."

I wanted desperately to believe Julian was not the son of some murderer, but I was having a hard time accepting that the general had not killed Vella in an attempt to take over Carabajel. I also badly wanted to tell him about the déjà vu. But I couldn't find the words to explain it all.

"Piper, is there something else?" Julian was looking at me, his eyebrows raised inquisitively.

I shook my head. "Nope."

"Listen, why don't you come to the palace with me?"

"That's nice of you, but I am too tired to move." Not to mention, there was no way I was going to the palace in my tattered state.

"Then can you sleep in your friend's room again tonight? Even with this weather, I don't trust Malfaedra."

"Can't you just post a watcher?" I asked. "Maybe there's one out there already."

"Right, good point," Julian said. "I should have thought of that. Does your head feel any better?"

I nodded.

"Good. Now make sure you bolt the door behind me. I'll come back first thing tomorrow morning. I'll bring two of the palace Humvees. You and your friends are going to have to evacuate and the palace is the safest place for you."

"Don't you need to ask your dad?"

"He won't care, believe me. You can have my entire wing, so I know you are safe."

Cecilia will be ecstatic, I thought. Talk about a fundraising opportunity.

I walked him to the door and another gust of wind hit us both in the face when he opened it.

He hugged me tightly. "Now lock the door and don't even think about pulling some Super Doll stunt. Promise?"

"I promise." I slammed the door behind him, using every ounce of strength I had. I bolted it again then collapsed mercifully on my bed and passed out.

Hours later, I woke with a start, panting from a vivid nightmare.

In my dream, I walked down to the pier behind the convent toward the flaming torch. This time, the man in the military uniform turned around. It was unmistakably the general, but his face was younger and unlined, and his hair was dark like Julian's.

He stepped toward me and reached for my left hand. He held it for a moment and then bent down on one knee and ever so slowly slipped a ring on my finger.

It was an enormous black diamond in the shape of a teardrop, set in a platinum band.

❦ 26 ❦

The Eve of the Storm

I thought I would have trouble falling back to sleep after the dream, but I didn't. I was out cold again even with all the lights still on, the wind howling, and the sea crashing.

When I woke up again, I looked at the clock and jumped out of bed so fast I almost caught my foot in the top sheet. It was nearly nine fifteen. Stupid me, I had completely forgotten to set the alarm. I was going to be late for class again.

And where was Julian?

In the shower, I tried to gather my thoughts. I wondered if it was possible the dream had not been a dream at all, but the déjà vu acting up again. If it was a dream, then it meant nothing. If it wasn't a dream, then was it possible the general had been in love with Vella and had planned to marry her? And if he was in love with her, then Julian was right. His father didn't kill her.

I thought back to what the general had said about the chateau. He told me he built it for a woman with a love of France. Vella was Icelandic, according to Malfaedra. Maybe she was Icelandic and loved France? And what was Malfaedra's problem then? All this time she had been waiting to possibly kill the general to avenge Vella's death when Vella and the general had been in love the whole time?

After my shower, I pulled on jeans and a black hoodie and winced at the sight of my sandals. They were covered with mucky, damp sand. I walked over to the balcony door to shake them out and gauge the wind, but when I slid the door open, I gasped. The waves had breached the seawall. Ocean rollers entirely covered the place where the saltwater pool had once been. The lounge chairs where Orchid had crept up on me were gone. The surf was now past the flagpole where I had collapsed.

We have got to get out of here, I thought. If the water had come up that far already and the storm had not even hit yet, then we were definitely not safe in the dormitory. I had kind of snickered when Julian said we could all go to the palace, but now it sounded like the idea of the century. Unless the Institute had a better plan, but given what my dad said about a confused woman sitting in an office in New York, I highly doubted it. I shook my sandals out as best I could, pulled them on, then raced for the door and sprinted to the lobby, keeping my head down to shield it from the wind mixed with driving rain.

When I opened the lobby door, the first thing I noticed was breakfast had not been set up. Damn, I thought. Even with my frayed nerves, I was still ravenous. I hadn't eaten a thing since lunch the day before.

I opened the door to the Reef Room and stopped. No one was there. The room was empty. I felt my hands start to shake and chewed at the edges of my thumb.

I couldn't imagine Cecilia would have left me behind, unless Aisling and Gareth said I was safe with Julian. But would they have really made that assumption when someone's safety was at risk? I didn't have the best impression of either Aisling or Gareth, but I doubted they would be cavalier about my whereabouts. I walked back into the lobby.

"Hello?" I called out. "Hola? Pilar?"

I headed down the hall to the kitchen, but it was vacant. The giant coffee urn was sitting abandoned on the counter next to empty pastry trays. Back in the lobby, I looked at the pay phone. Even if it worked, I couldn't fathom what I would tell my father. *Hi Dad, I'm fine, but everyone else is gone, and I'm the only one here at a school that is flooding*. No way. I didn't need to panic the man.

I pushed the lobby door open and looked across the parking lot at Cecilia's dormitory. It was on slightly higher ground than our buildings, so perhaps they were all hiding out in her room. It was worth a try. I made a run for it, feeling raindrops pounding my back. A palm frond as large as a car was blowing around like a feather. I had to duck twice to avoid it hitting me in the face.

But when I got to Cecilia's dorm, the door to her building was locked. "No, no," I whispered. I pulled on the door and rattled it back and forth. But there was no question about it. The door was locked and bolted.

"I cannot believe they left me here. I cannot believe it," I said. I felt tears burning in my eyes. I was exhausted, my head hurt, and I was starving. How could they leave a student for dead with a hurricane on its way? Now I had no choice but to wait for Julian and pray in the midst of everything going on with his father, he had not forgotten about me too.

I turned around and pressed my back against the glass door. The only explanation I could come up with was they had indeed assumed I was safe with Julian. After all, Aisling and Gareth had seen me with him. They didn't know he was the general's son, but they knew he was a Carabajelian who was supposedly living on the school grounds for the summer. They probably figured I had driven off with him the night before.

I raced back across the parking lot and up the stairs to my room. I was panting and soaked by the time I managed to dig my keys out of my pocket.

When I pushed the door open, I saw the note. I had somehow missed it in my rush to get to class. Silly me for even thinking there was class with a major storm on the horizon.

Piper, I am very worried and hope you are okay. We knocked on your door several times this morning. I would have come in to check on you, but Pilar is gone and she took the master keys. We all hope you are with a local friend as Aisling said you might be. If you are still here, please use the pay phone, dial zero, and tell the operator you need a taxi. I will pay him upon your arrival. We have been evacuated to the airport. xo, Cecilia.

I slid down to the floor with my back against the closet. The pay phone? Was she serious? Didn't she know the thing was broken almost every day? And call a taxi? Didn't she know there were only two of them? Given the meltdown the last driver had, I doubted he'd ever come back.

I counted to ten and tried to calm myself down. Julian just had to come back for me. He promised he would.

I didn't know what to do with myself while I waited, but packing a bag seemed like a logical decision given the scenario. If I was going to ride the storm out in the airport or the palace, I was going to need more than jeans and a sweatshirt.

I pulled my backpack down from the hook inside the closet and stuffed it with clean underwear, a night-shirt, and two tank tops. Then I reached for my makeup bag and my journal, which was still damp, and put those inside too. I was about to zip the backpack closed when there was a knock on my door. I dropped the backpack and rushed to unlock it.

"Julian, thank God," I said as I swung the door open.

Fernando stood in the hallway wearing a furious expression. He grabbed my arm and pulled me toward him as he sprayed something into the air from a small canister. I tried to push him away from me, but the smell was so potent, I could barely breathe. Then everything went black.

27

Vella's Bedroom

I woke up slowly. My eyelids felt heavy, so heavy I could barely open them, but I fought the need to sleep more. When I finally managed to shake off my stupor, I propped myself up on my elbows. My palms were sweaty and my mouth was dry.

I looked around deliriously. I was lying on a four-poster bed, and everything in the room was gold—the bedspread on top of me, a dresser with an oval mirror above it, and the chaise lounge in the corner. Even the moldings on the walls were covered in a gilded metallic paint. Thick gold drapery concealed two windows, and I could hear the driving rain hitting the glass behind the curtains.

I didn't need time to ponder my whereabouts. The fragrant vapor of the incense told me enough. An urn sat on top of the dresser, a plume of smoke wafting through an opening in the lid.

All I could recall was Fernando had knocked on my door and sprayed something in my face. But I couldn't remember anything else.

I pushed the covers back and stood up on shaky legs. I tiptoed over to the window and pulled back the curtains. One of the windows was cracked open ever so slightly letting in fresh air and dampness from the rain. I tried to push it open farther, but my strength was zapped.

The room looked out over the pier and I could see the waves were still gigantic. The tide had almost reached the top of the wall where the beach gate stood.

I let the curtains fall back over the window, and I walked to the dresser. My survival instinct was telling me I had to somehow extinguish the urn. I pulled my shirt up to cover my nose, and I pried off the lid. Five tiny tea candles burned under a slotted tray filled with potpourri.

The smell was overpowering, but I managed to blow out all but one tea candle. I hurried back over to the window and pulled the curtains aside to breathe in the fresh air again. Then I went back to the urn, took a deep breath, and extinguished the last candle. I coughed a little, put the lid back on, and then returned to the window. A hairclip was jammed in the window to keep it open a few inches. How strange, I thought. If they were trying to drug me, why did they give me fresh air?

I sat back down on the edge of the bed and tried to form my thoughts into a coherent plan. I could wait patiently for someone to appear—Malfaedra presumably—and determine what she wanted. Or I could try to escape like I did the last time. Waiting was not a viable option. What if they were planning to hypnotize me into a Black Mariah? But escaping was also impossible. Even if I got outside, I would be running into the start of a hurricane. And where would I go anyway? The beach had washed away, and I assumed the school had flooded too.

I reclined against the pillows and felt my eyes closing again. The horrid incense was still lingering, and it was making me light-headed. I feared I was going to pass out again. My chest was starting to feel tight and my head was getting hazy. I sat up, then collapsed back onto the bed.

Fight, Piper, fight, I said to myself. Don't sleep. You can't go to sleep. I felt like I was drunk, and I had only ever been drunk once before. Jamie brought a bottle of vodka to the base library one night, and we took turns sipping it as we restocked the shelves. Then I had careened home on foot and passed out on my bed. My dad and Becky were clueless about the whole episode. They actually believed I had overexerted myself lifting books in the reference room.

I was about to shift my body into an upright position again when Malfaedra's rhythmic voice said from somewhere, "It is no use, darling."

My eyes flew open as Malfaedra appeared at the foot of the bed.

"Stop fighting it, Piper," she said in her breathy voice. "You are home now."

"No," I protested. "I am not home."

"How do you like being in your room again?" she asked.

"What do you mean?"

"Your bedroom. You recognize it, of course. Sit up and look."

She strolled over to a door on the opposite side of the room and opened it. It was a large walk-in closet filled with shimmering black gowns.

"I don't know what you are talking about," I said.

She turned to me with a wicked expression on her face. Her violet eyes had darkened to a deep purple and the curve of her jawbones protruded a little as she clenched her teeth. Even hateful, she was drop-dead gorgeous. My stomach tightened into a ball because something about her face suddenly looked familiar, something about the way she blinked and narrowed her eyes.

"I have waited for this moment for a very long time," she said.

"What do you want?" I asked. "Even if I am reincarnated, what could it possibly matter now?"

"I told you about the prophecy."

"Yes," I said. "But even if I am Vella, I am not here to destroy anyone."

She folded her arms. "Don't insult my high intelligence. Of course, you are not."

"I'm confused," I whispered.

"When I return, you will die. You said it and you weren't talking about the general and his loyalists. I just led everyone to believe that was the case. Even you last night, since your amnesia has not fully subsided."

"I still don't get it Malfaedra. I'm sorry. The incense is really strong. Can you open a window or something? I can't think clearly."

"Don't pretend you don't know. Don't play innocent. I have waited twenty years for this moment, and once you tell me where it is, I am going to kill you for a second time."

"*You* killed Vella?"

"Good heavens. Let me refresh your failing memory. When you said, 'When I return, you will die,' you meant me. You meant I will die." She shrugged. "It was so easy to blame the general for your death. The whole island believes me. The other Black Mariahs believe me."

I stared at her in dread. Julian was right. She was way more deranged than anyone believed. And a murderess.

"You see, Vella," Malfaedra continued, "or Piper, if you prefer that ghastly name, I have been preparing myself for years to meet you upon your return. Planning and preparing. So, I will ask you again. Where is it?"

"Where is what?" I asked.

"The hellir. The cave of black diamonds. Think. Reach into your past life and tell me."

"I really don't know what you are talking about."

"Then think. Remember, breathe in the incense and return to the past."

"I don't even know what a hellir is."

"Of course, you do! Hellir is your language. The cave. The cave of black diamonds. I have searched for it. I have searched high and low, but I cannot find the entrance. You are the only one who knows where it is. You discovered it because of your tiresome flowers."

All I could think about was the ring in my dream. The black diamond in the shape of a teardrop.

"You know what those diamonds mean for us. They stand to be the rarest gemstones on the planet. When I find the cave, we will export the diamonds and I will rule this lava rock once and for all."

The general knows where they are too, I thought.

He must. If my dream was real, he must know the location of the cave. He made a ring from the diamond. For Vella. Or, and I shuddered at the thought, for me.

Malfaedra pushed me back against the pillows. She reached into a fold in her gown and retrieved a miniature sword with a bejeweled handle. She leaned over me and I felt the metal against my throat.

"Tell me," she said with ice in her voice. "Tell me or it won't be poison like the last time. It will be a quick little cut to your throat."

A banging noise coming from the other side of the door cut her off and Malfaedra turned her head toward the sound. "What now?" she hissed.

As she walked toward the door, I rolled out of the bed and stood up with my last remaining bit of strength. I grabbed the urn and held it with one hand, poised to strike. It was the only weapon I had. She spun back around and looked at me.

"What do you think you are doing, stupid girl?" she yelled.

The pounding on the door continued, but she took a step toward me, and I threw the urn in her direction, hitting her shoulder. She faltered momentarily but regained her footing and charged at me with her tiny sword knife. She grabbed me by my dreadlocks and pushed me down. I felt the cold blade against my neck.

"Tell me where it is so I can kill you off like I did the

last—" She never finished the sentence because the door to the room burst open. The general stood in the doorway with Julian right behind him.

"Piper!" Julian cried.

"What do you think you are doing here?" Malfaedra hollered.

She released her grip on me and straightened up, her face furious. "You," she said. At first, I didn't know who she meant, but then I saw her eyes were burning into the general's.

He moved toward her, and she forgot all about me and Julian. Julian catapulted across the bed and put his arms around me.

"Piper, I'm so sorry! I never should have left you alone. When I tried to return this morning, the roads were flooded. We had to drive through the brush, and it took way longer than I expected."

"They drugged me. The incense," I stammered. "It's a tranquilizer."

"You're okay now, I promise. I won't let anything happen to you."

He helped me to my feet and shoved the window open before pushing me behind him.

Malfaedra stood there with her knife poised, looking mildly amused. "Perfect," she said. "I'm going to kill all of you. Three fools at once."

"Let them be, Malfaedra. They're kids," the general

said rather patiently, considering we were evidently at the mercy of a madwoman.

"She is more than that and you know it," Malfaedra said. She placed her knife on the dresser and bent down. I remembered the pistol strapped to her ankle boot.

"She has a gun!" I warned, but it was too late. She had already retrieved it from under her gown and was pointing it squarely at the general's head.

"Finally, I have a clear shot at you," Malfaedra said. "How long I have waited for you to be free of your guards and your armored trucks and your security force. I knew one day I would be able to kill you, but I never thought you'd walk through my door."

"Julian, leave with Ruth," the general said.

"They'll leave all right. In one of our fine ebony caskets," Malfaedra said. She waved her gun carelessly at us.

"Malfaedra," the general said in a soft voice. "Let it be. Please, let it be."

"Why should I? This girl is the only key to the diamond mine. She will lead me to it, and then you will all die."

"I already know where it is, Malfaedra," he said.

She lowered the gun. "What did you say?"

"I said I know where the diamond mine is."

"You are lying."

"Vella told me."

"No, she didn't."

"Yes, she did."

Malfaedra shook her head furiously. "She didn't tell you where it is. She wanted to keep it a secret for the Black Mariahs. She was loyal to us. I thought she would tell me once I poisoned her. I thought when she knew she was dying she would tell me."

"She killed Vella?" Julian asked me, and I nodded.

"Shut your mouth, boy," Malfaedra said.

"Julian, please. Give me a minute here," the general said. "It doesn't matter now, Malfaedra. What's done is done."

"But why would she have told you and not me? I was her sister in faith."

"We have been mining it for years."

"I don't believe you," she bellowed. "You only let me stay because you thought one of these days, I would be the one to find it."

"That is not true. You know why I let you stay."

"I loathe you," she said. "Killing you will be my salvation."

"I doubt that," the general replied.

"Is that so, you coward? Well, why don't you tell him the truth then?" She nodded in the direction of Julian. "Tell him the real reason why you let me stay."

"Julian, go," the general said. "Take care of Ruth."

"Tell him!" she shrieked. "Tell him why you let me live here and carry on as I do."

The general looked from Malfaedra to us and back

to her again. But before he could say a word, it hit me. The chiseled jawline. The high cheekbones. The thick, glossy black hair. I glanced at Julian, but he was waiting for his father to speak.

"Because," the general said with great resignation. "Because you are the mother of my son."

❦ 28 ❧

Escape from Carabajel

Julian stared at his father and Malfaedra in shock. When he turned to me, his eyes searched mine for an answer. I knew he was asking me wordlessly if I had known the secret. I shook my head.

"Papa?" Julian asked incredulously.

"It is true, Julian."

Malfaedra cocked the trigger of the gun. She aimed it at the general's forehead again, and a sinister laugh escaped from her lips. "You idiot," she said. "What we could have been."

The general folded his arms across his chest. He was still eerily calm, considering he was yet again staring directly into the barrel of a gun.

"Go, Julian," he said. "For the last time, leave and take Ruth with you."

"I'm not leaving you. Piper, you run." Julian dragged me around Malfaedra and propelled me into the hall.

"You'd best go too, Julian," Malfaedra said, "unless you want to watch your father die."

As I regained my footing in the hallway, I caught the first whiff of smoke. To my right, there was a banister leading to a spiral staircase. And sure enough, a cloud of smoke was rising up the stairwell. I assumed at first it was incense until I inhaled and realized it was just plain smoke. From a fire.

I stepped back into the room and tugged on Julian's sleeve. "Um, Julian, fire," I said.

"What?" he asked.

"I think the convent is on fire."

I wasn't sure if Malfaedra had heard me. She was standing as close to the general as the pointed gun would allow, and she did not turn her head. Neither did the general.

Something crashed beneath us. It sounded like a wall had collapsed.

Malfaedra lowered the gun. "What in the hell was that? Who did you bring with you? My guards have their orders. To kill if necessary!"

"No one is getting killed here," the general said.

"I believe the convent is on fire," I said. I tried to

keep my voice steady. Everyone looked at me. "El convento está en llamas," I tried.

"Julian, get out of here." The general muscled him toward the door and slammed it closed behind us. We both heard the latch lock.

"Christ almighty," Julian said. He banged on the door with his fist. "Papa, open this door!"

I looked down the hallway and then sucked in my breath and reached for Julian's hand. The spiral staircase was starting to collapse, leaving a smoldering black hole in its place.

"The staircase is gone!" I said, but Julian was still hammering on the door.

"Damn it, Papa, open this door!"

"Julian, we have to find another way down. Your father, Malfaedra, they'll get out. There is obviously something, um, clearly, between them."

Julian looked at me with a stunned expression. "This is unbelievable."

"I know."

"Julian? Julian?" A male voice was calling his name, and we turned to see two of the general's guards appear at the opposite end of the hall from the missing staircase.

"What is going on?" the taller of the two asked when they approached us.

"We found Piper, but my father is stuck behind this door with that lunatic woman and she has a gun!"

"Get out of here, Julian," the guard said. "The convent is on fire. We'll get the general. Take the stairs to the left."

Julian didn't budge.

The second guard said, "Julian, get the lady out of here at least. We'll help your father."

Julian rubbed his temples, thinking. Then he said, "Nicolas, Damian, thank you. Gracias."

Julian took my hand and pulled me forward into a sprinting run. Almost immediately, we both started hacking and coughing from the rising smoke.

When we reached the other end of the hall, there was a staircase just as the guard had said. It looked narrow and steep. Julian touched the metal railing with the back of his hand.

"Be careful, it's hot," he said. "And pull your shirt up over your nose and mouth."

He gripped my hand tighter, and we descended the steps as fast as we could manage without losing our balance. When we reached the first floor, I saw we were at one end of the Hall of Mirrors. Which meant the door I had come in with Orchid was somewhere farther down on the right. Or was it the left?

"This way, and keep holding my hand," Julian said, leading me in the opposite direction from the way I would have chosen.

"Wait, are you sure?" I asked. "I think the door is that way."

"This door is closer," he said. "We came in this way. My father knows this place inside and out."

The moment the words came out of his mouth, we heard a gunshot.

"Oh God," Julian said and turned back toward the staircase.

"Julian, you can't go up there! It's not safe. Look at the stairs." The support beam holding up the staircase we had descended was wobbling precariously.

"Run before it falls on top of us!" he said.

We took off down the Hall of Mirrors. I was still holding his hand tightly when a piece of wood tripped me and sent me careening toward the marble floor. I managed to grab the edge of one of the mirrors, and I felt Julian's arms go around me as I steadied myself.

I began to cough uncontrollably as Julian rushed us toward a door and kicked it open with his foot. We were in a chapel but not the same one I had stumbled upon the day before. This one was darker and smaller. Candles flickered from sconces, and statues of expressionless nuns wearing the habits of the Black Mariahs were set in small niches every few feet against both walls. I smelled the incense immediately and looked up. Crystal chandeliers with smoking urns set in the center of the lamps dangled above us.

I gasped for air, but my lungs were burning.

"Are you okay?" Julian asked.

"I think so."

"We should have put an end to these nuns long ago. But my father..." his cracked voice trailed off.

"He'll make it," I said. "She won't kill him if she used to love him." I hoped what I was saying was true.

When he didn't move, I said, "Julian, we can't breathe in this incense. It's some kind of sedative."

"The exit is there," he said, pointing to a side door.

We covered our mouths again and ran down the center aisle of the chapel. Julian pushed the door open, and as soon as he did, we were finally outside. We huddled together against the cold stone of the convent and caught our breaths. The wind and rain were swirling about us furiously.

"Is this the hurricane?" I asked between gasps.

"No, it hasn't even started."

"What time is it?" I had no idea how long I had been locked in the convent.

"Jesus, of all the things to be concerned about," he said, but he looked at his watch anyway. "It's almost one thirty. Which means we have to leave right now. Look over there." He pointed to a large vehicle parked against the tree line at the edge of the property. "Do you see the Humvee?"

"Yes."

"That's ours. On the count of three, we are going to run for it, okay?"

"Okay."

"One," he yelled, "two, three!"

We tried sprinting, but the ground was slippery, and twice I almost lost my balance and had to grab Julian's arm.

When we got to the Humvee, Julian reached behind the bumper and pulled out a hidden set of keys. The truck beeped as he unlocked the doors, and I scrambled into the passenger seat as he got behind the wheel. He locked the doors behind us, started the engine, and then gripped the steering wheel with both hands.

"Did my father really say what I think he said?" he asked. "Did he really say Malfaedra is my mother? That maniac is my mother?"

"Your faces," I murmured. "They are so similar. I noticed it when you were both in the room."

"How is it possible?" he asked.

"Julian, I'm so sorry. I really have no earthly clue."

"My father always said my mother died right after I was born from the dysentery epidemic."

I touched his arm but was speechless. What could I say to someone who just found out his mother was a brainwashing killer nun?

"It's unreal. Truly unreal," Julian said as he put the Humvee in gear. He started driving toward a road no wider than an old-fashioned wagon trail.

"Wait," I said. "Where are you going? What about your father?" I had assumed we were just going to wait until the guards and the general came out. *That is, if they did come out.* I cowered at the thought.

"Believe me, I don't want to leave, but I've got to get you to the airport. And Nicolas and Damian are armed. They'll do what they have to do."

"The airport? But why?" Something flashed on my right and I turned in my seat. "Oh no," I said. "Look!" I pointed to the convent. Flames were shooting out of the windows of the upper floors. "Do you think the other nuns got out?" I asked.

"I hope so," Julian replied. "We didn't see any of them when we came in. They may have evacuated because of the storm, although I have no idea where they would go. Their guards are missing too. We expected to have trouble coming in, but the door was open."

I slumped in my seat, overcome suddenly by a mind-boggling wave of guilt. I had been so drugged by the incense it had not entirely occurred to me that the general, Julian, and their guards had come to the convent to get me out. If the general ended up killed, it was all my fault.

"Julian, I'm so sorry. Your dad. You guys came for me."

He reached for my hand. "Don't be sorry. You didn't make us come and get you."

"But how did you even know I was there?"

"I went back to the school to pick you and your friends up to bring you to the palace, but everyone was gone. There was massive miscommunication, but we eventually got a straight answer from some of the observers that the school had been evacuated to the airport. So, I drove out there to make sure you were okay. When I got there, your friends said they thought you were with me. Naturally, I panicked and drove back to the palace. And wouldn't you know it, but a Black Mariah was there. She'd made it halfway up the mountain before one of our men found her. She said you had been kidnapped."

"A Black Mariah warned you about me?"

"Yeah, imagine that."

"What was her name?" I asked, even though I already guessed the answer.

"It was a flower. Tulip or something."

"Orchid," I said. I couldn't believe she went to such great lengths to help me.

"You know her?"

"She's the one Malfaedra sent to befriend me."

"Well, she saved you," he said. "She said she propped the window open in the room where you were being kept so you wouldn't inhale too much of the narcotic."

I felt tears well up in my eyes. Even poor Orchid ended up involved in the mess.

"She did save me. She used a hair clip to keep the window open. The fresh air thinned out the incense, and then I was able to blow out the urn. But you saved me too. And your father."

"Don't mention it," Julian said.

"Thank you," I managed, even though those two words didn't seem like enough.

Julian held my hand as he accelerated and drove fast down a steep trail. The Humvee lurched to the left and to the right, so I gripped the handrail on the door. When we finally reached the edge of the woods, Julian made a right turn and I recognized the road as the one leading to the school.

"I need to thank her too," I finally said.

"I'll tell her for you."

"Is she still at the palace?"

"Yes, she was drenched and weak, so our staff set her up in one of the guest bedrooms. But we can't go there now because I've got to get you to the airport."

"Julian, I would rather stay with you, help you with your father, and thank Orchid. I don't need to be with my classmates right now."

"I want nothing more than that too, Piper, but you have friends in high places."

"What do you mean?"

"The father of one of your classmates sent a private jet to bring you all back to the States."

"Omigod. Whose father?"

"I don't know. When I went to the airport, they told me the plane would be leaving at two. A girl begged me to find you. She was very sweet. She said her father sent the plane and she was your best friend and she didn't want to leave without you."

"Coco," I guessed. "Her father sent a jet?"

"Apparently."

"You can't make me leave you."

He squeezed my hand tighter. "I have to, Piper. They are saying this is a Category Five storm. Carabajel City and our coastal communities could be wiped out. I can't have you stay here on the island when there is a private jet waiting to take you home. Even your father knows about it."

"My father? How do you know all of this?"

Julian swerved to avoid a puddle. The road was so flooded in places, I was certain the engine was going to stall. Every jolt of the vehicle pained me. My lungs felt singed, and I had the worst taste imaginable in my mouth from the smoke. And now Julian was telling me I was going to have to board an airplane? In this weather?

"Your teacher was so worried. She told me if I found you to tell you your father had been notified about the plane."

"Come with me then," I said.

A smile formed at the corner of his mouth, and he looked at me sadly. "Piper, I have to go back and help my father."

"But I don't want to leave you."

"I can't believe you want to stay after all that has happened to you here. You were the innocent party. This island has always been filled with madness."

"Did you ever ask your father for his side of the story?"

"Yes, I demanded that my father explain everything as we drove to the convent. He confirmed Vella had mystical gardening powers, and that she eradicated the dysentery epidemic from the island. He also admitted she was the one who discovered the black sugar and the black diamonds. She told him all her secrets right before she died. He swore he didn't kill her. He said she died from mysterious causes."

"Now we know the mysterious cause was Malfaedra," I said.

Julian glanced sideways at me and shook his head in disgust.

The road in front of us opened up to a long, empty stretch, and Julian stepped on the gas harder and started to drive at breakneck speed.

"I also asked Clara what the hell she was doing giving you the rosary. She said she wanted to warn you the Black Mariahs hide behind religious purity, but she lost her nerve before she got the words out."

"She meant well."

"Clara said she couldn't believe it when she saw you sitting there in the dining room. She said she was certain Vella had returned from the dead."

Something occurred to me. "How long has Clara worked for your father?" I asked.

"I don't know. Forever. Gosh, since before I was born."

"I think they were in love," I said.

"Clara and my father!"

"No, sorry, I meant Vella and your father."

"What makes you think that?"

"I had an epiphany of sorts. A dream."

"Oh, Christ, Piper, the incense has gotten to you."

"No, really. Ask Clara. Ask Clara who the palace was built for. I think your father built it for Vella."

"Fine, but if he loved Vella, how did he end up with Malfaedra?"

We were approaching the wall of Carabajel City, and when I looked down the abandoned main street, I couldn't believe only a few weeks had passed since I arrived. The street party had been in full swing that night. Now the gaslights burned alone, tiny flames blinking in the rain.

"Listen, I really want to stay with you to figure the rest of it out," I said.

"Piper." His voice was grave. "I want you to be safe. I'll find a way for us to be together again. Either here in Carabajel or in the States. I promise."

We drove along in silence. When we exited downtown, we headed toward the rotary where the drenched statue of Vella looked skyward into the storm. I could see the airport control tower up ahead and the bright light of the rotating beacon making a slow circle against the gray sky.

Julian drove straight across the grass and stopped as close as he could to the runway. The clock on the dashboard said one forty-four. A few men in uniform ran toward the Humvee, but when they saw it was Julian who jumped out of the driver's side, they stopped in their tracks and bowed down.

"Stop the jet!" Julian yelled. One of the men turned around and went running toward the tarmac, leaping over a hedge in the process.

Julian held my hand as we ran together in the direction of the runway. The small jet was parked about a hundred feet from the circular fountain with the goldfish that had been the first thing that looked familiar the day I arrived.

A flight attendant was just pulling up the rear jet stairs, but she stopped and lowered them again when she saw the airport guard running toward her with Julian and me right on his tail. When we reached the plane, we were both out of breath, but Julian pulled me into his arms anyway and kissed me.

"Super Doll," he whispered, "I think it was love at first sight."

"I think it was love at first sight for me too." I felt hot tears start to burn in my eyes.

"We'll figure it out. I'll come to the States. Wait for me."

"Thank you for saving me. And thank your father too. I know he will be okay."

I knew everyone was watching from the airplane windows, but I didn't care. Julian kissed me again, and then he put his hands on my lower back and helped me up the stairs. The flight attendant smiled sympathetically, as if a little island romance was ending. If only she knew it was so much more.

"Wait," Julian called out.

I turned around, embarrassed by the tears running down my face.

"I almost forgot." He handed me a black velvet pouch. "My father said I should give this to you. Consider it a promise you will see me again."

Cecilia appeared in the aircraft doorway behind the flight attendant. "Piper, are you all right?" she asked, alarmed.

"Yes, thank you."

I gripped the pouch and kissed Julian one last time before I tripped up the slick metal jet stairs. I turned around when I reached the top, and Julian, flanked by airport security, held up one hand in farewell as the flight attendant pulled up the stairs and closed the aircraft door.

My classmates were all turned backward in their seats, looking at me with a mixture of interest and relief.

Cecilia put her arm around me. "Where have you been? We were so worried about you."

"Long story," I replied.

"I understand. You can explain everything later."

"Where are we going?" I asked.

"Miami. The Institute is working on giving us a temporary location stateside."

As she turned to take her seat, I reached for her arm. "Thank you for waiting, Cecilia," I said. "I'm really sorry I caused so much trouble."

She hugged me. "It's okay. We're just so glad you're safe. I didn't know how I was going to explain to your father we left you on Carabajel."

The flight attendant came up behind me, interrupting us. "Your seat is here, sweetheart." She pointed to a solo seat on the left-hand side of the plane and handed me a cashmere blanket.

Cecilia walked forward and took a seat in the front row next to Coco, who caught my eye.

"Piper," she called. "You all right?"

I nodded. "And thanks, Coco. For the plane."

She smiled. "No worries."

I looked out the window. Julian was still standing there watching us. I waved, but I knew he couldn't see me through the tiny oval window covered in raindrops.

"Are you sure you're all right, Piper?" Gemma asked. She was sitting diagonally across from me next to Bronwyn.

"Yes. Thanks. Sorry I held us up."

"You didn't. We only got takeoff clearance five minutes ago so don't worry."

I smiled at her gratefully and took one last look at Julian as the plane taxied down the runway. The takeoff and ascent were rougher than I ever could have imagined was possible. I only had a second to catch one last glimpse of Carabajel before the clouds hindered my view of the island. Even the rotating beacon disappeared.

I wiped my face with an edge of the blanket. It occurred to me I was traveling without identification. No purse, no passport, nothing. Everything was still in my room at the dorm. The Air Force would just have to bail me out of this one, I thought.

I closed my eyes and didn't open them again until I felt a ray of sunlight warm my face. I looked out the window and saw the clouds were thick beneath us, but the sky around us was a perfect shade of blue.

What an insane island, I mused, even if it had sort of been a grand adventure. And to think I almost believed all the talk of reincarnation and past lives.

I prayed the general got away from Malfaedra. I didn't even want to think about the gunshot we had heard.

Once the turbulence settled down, I looked around to make sure no one was watching me. Only then did I reach into my pocket to take out the pouch Julian had given me. I untied it and looked inside. I didn't see anything at first, so I turned it over and felt something hard and cold drop into my open hand.

A black teardrop diamond set in a platinum band gleamed in my palm.

The End

ACKNOWLEDGMENTS

Thank you so very much to the following: my mom, whose artwork graces the cover and who has the miraculous ability to make my characters come alive in art; my dad, whose business brought me to the enchanting islands of the Caribbean when I was a little girl; the Prospect Reef Resort on Tortola; British West Indies Airways; William Beetle; my editors William Harrison and Judy Roth; DartFrog Books; and Jean-Claude Lanza, who has been everything to me.

ABOUT THE AUTHOR

Erin Schulz is an American writer from Newport, Rhode Island. She holds a baccalaureate in history from Fordham University and a postgraduate degree in international affairs from American University's School of International Service. She is also a graduate of the Swiss finishing school, Institut Villa Pierrefeu. She lives in Florida.

www.superdollthenovel.com